FATHER REIGN

Michael Tobin

ISBN: 979-8-9926037-0-5

LCCN: 2025903291

Book Cover by Nicholas Tobin.

First edition, 2025.

For Family

1

Rain

Rain crashed against the glass and poured downwards into the crevices of the aged brick building. It was the kind of rain that comes in waves, ranging from a steady stream to a visibility shattering downpour. The never-ending kind of rain that occasionally brings hope of ceasing only to steal that hope as it begins to bellow up again. There was no thunder to break up the noise of its steady drowning fall. The rain remained an omnipresent white noise, ringing in the ears. At the bottom of the building, puddles had long since formed. A mixture of water and asphalt slowly churning as more rain came to reinforce the growing pools. The creation was mesmerizing, enough for someone to stare into it and lose their sense of being. Forgetting dreams, ambitions, and loved ones, just fixated on the pool of despair, and feeling helpless as drops of rain aid the madness.

Working with the rain were the clouds. Forming a gray forcefield against the sun's rays that endlessly proved impenetrable. As strong as the rays were, the mass of gray defeated them with hardly an effort. They cast a shroud of darkness over the drenched land and the aged brick building that stood on it. It was the kind of gloom that even the most optimistic would find hopeless. The rain and the clouds seemed to soak the souls out of all the people that day. There were no umbrellas, no rain jackets, no headlights patrolling the streets. Those unfortunate enough to be dressed in this heinous atmosphere had long since retreated to their homes, yearning for an end to the day. They were still hopeless, however, as the constant patter of raindrops reminded them of the looming threat.

The lack of life on the streets did not only include people. Animals cowered in trees, tunnels, and brush as the rainfall continued. Two white eggs sat on the roof of the gray building, the wind and rain inching them treacherously closer to the edge. The building stood high. A fall from this height would surely end the lives of the doves inside before they had even begun. This was the kind of rain that made one believe such a fate may be for the best. A creature taking its first breath in a place like this would surely be on the wrong side of destiny.

Inside the third floor of the building a man paced back and forth. His gait was not frantic, it was one of thought and conflict. For all that was going on outside the building, it was clear that the man was focused on what was going on inside his head. He offered not even a glance at the room's single rain drenched window. His arms were crossed, with one of his hands up to his chin in contemplation. His shirt, checkered blue and green, was hastily buttoned, evidenced by the buttonless hole that sat near his neck. His pants were drenched at the bottoms after splashing through puddles in front of the building. His soaked leather loafers had seen the brunt of the damage, leaving prints on the tile floor as he walked back and forth across the room.

The room was dimly lit. The only illumination was a cone shaped light hanging from the middle of the ceiling, and the gray that came from the window. The room looked bare, having one table in the middle and a chair off to the side. There were a few cabinets on the sides of the room, but it appeared those were only for show. There was one closed doorway into the room with a steel handle and no window. This was a room meant for waiting in limbo. A room that brought no comfort, only the hanging shadow of doubt for what news would be brought to the waiting patient. A place where the line between uncertainty and reality becomes blurred as a person ponders how the next words they hear may change their lives drastically.

On the table sat a woman. She sat slumped with her eyes staring longingly at the pointless cabinets. Her chestnut-colored hair fell past her shoulders as it slowly dried out from the shower she received walking into the building. She wore a soaked pink dress and white shoes that were beginning to turn as gray as the sky. Her face held an expression of fear, her mouth hanging open and her lip beginning to quiver. It was the look of a patient who was living in uncertainty while awaiting the news. She was already picturing how her life would unfold after hearing the terrible words that would be uttered next. The dark room seemed to hold less hope than the world that was being assaulted by rain outside.

The steel handle on the door suddenly turned and the eyes in the room darted towards it in anticipation. All emotions were wiped clean as the door began to swing open, ears perked up ready to listen. A gaunt man in a white coat slowly entered the room with a look on his face that was difficult to read. It was the look of a man who had something to say, something that may be upsetting. The look also exuded an air of repetition. This was a man who had time and time again delivered news and seen emotions ranging from tears of joy to tears of pain. He slowly and methodically closed the door behind him and turned to face the other two in the room. He gave each of them a look for a second before settling his eyes on the woman.

"Mr. and Mrs. Francis," the man in the coat began, "I know that this has been a long and difficult journey for both of you. When two people find love it is only natural that they wish to create something together. Far too often I see couples like you who can't accomplish this naturally. I am sorry to tell you that you are not pregnant Mrs. Francis."

The woman averted her gaze from the man in the coat back to the useless shelves on the side of the room. Her mouth continued to be held open, as she unblinkingly realized what had become her reality. She thought that she had prepared herself for this news, but the words still struck her like a sword hitting a chopping block. This was nothing new to her. She had been trying to have a child with her husband for the past two years. The two visited countless doctor's offices just like this one, only to repeatedly hear the same tale. At first, she felt shame at not being able to conceive. She and her husband told themselves that the inability was a fluke, and that they would surely be able to have a child the next try.

After several more failed attempts, the shame turned into anger. It was an irrational anger directed towards herself that evolved into fury against her husband and her loved ones. She did not know why this was happening to her, why she was not able to have the child that she yearned for her whole life. Among her first memories were playing with dolls in her large pink playhouse and having the dolls raise children of their own. She was angry that she had been robbed of this special gift that even the inanimate were granted. This anger turned her hostile towards everyone around her, and for many months she was unable to leave the house. Her blood would boil over with rage whenever she saw another young mother gleefully raising their child, forming the bond that she would never be able to craft.

The anger finally transitioned into numbness. At first this evolution was to the relief of her husband and loved ones, but then turned to their dismay. It seemed that the months of anger leeched the very soul from the woman. At least when the woman was fuming, it was evident that she was still there, feeling her emotions deeply. Once the numbness set in, the woman became a shell of a person. She would go through her daily routines without issue, but those who loved her could tell in her eyes that she would never truly be satisfied.

This was the numbness in which the woman sat with while staring into space. Her mouth still hung open, but she had nothing to say. Her husband looked at her longingly, hoping for any sort of reaction. He had been with her throughout this turbulent journey of trying to conceive a child. It was never a life goal of his to have a child, until he discovered how desperately his wife wanted one. He loved his wife, and hearing her go on about the joyous things she would do as a mother made him dream of the future that they could share as a family. They would travel around the world, seeing the great pyramids of Giza, the lush green forests of South America, and walk the length of the Great Wall of China. He had never known that he wanted to do these things, but now he too felt robbed of the adventures that he would not get to enjoy with his family.

The man did not feel the same anger and hatred that his wife felt after the repeated failures. He tried to be accepting of the circumstances, attempting to appreciate the things that he did have in his life. He was still married to a beautiful woman and had a successful career as an architect. As the rejections added up, it became more difficult to love what he had. There was the pressure coming from his angered wife. Whenever he tried to comfort her, she would become agitated and push him further away. She had become a person whom he did not know. His parents too began to pressure him. They were getting older, and they wished to have a grandchild. He thought about the things he could have done differently to change where life had led him.

The doctor began talking about other options for having a child. The man knew that this was pointless, he and his wife tuned out the doctor as soon as he delivered the result. Adoption, surrogacy, or any other method would not do. The woman dreamed her whole life about experiencing every part of motherhood, savoring equally the joys and pains that raising a child required. She felt that if she did not experience the burden of carrying the fetus and subsequent agony of childbirth then she would not be able to form as strong of a bond with the child. The man pleaded with her that the bond would be nonetheless secure, but the woman would not budge. She knew what she wanted.

The doctor finished delivering the news as he had done countless times before. The couple too had heard this speech many times, and without a word began to leave another torture filled room.

"We have extra ponchos downstairs if you need," said the doctor, noticing that the two had not yet dried from their walk into the building. "It is getting pretty bad out there."

Creation

The man sat silently in a room equipped with a large oak cabinet and a polished oak desk positioned with a view out of the window. The window was being battered by wind and drops of water, but there was hardly a sound in this room. The room was well decorated with accolades that the man achieved throughout his years. He had been hailed as one of the great young architectural minds in the country and had the achievements to go with it.

The man developed his love for architecture as a young boy working with his father. In the mornings, they would get up and watch the sun rise and begin to work together. His father owned a quaint woodshop that operated as the main source of furniture for the small town that they lived in. People would come from all over the town to get chairs, beds, cabinets, and more. The man always loved that whenever he went to a neighboring house he would feel as if he was already a part of it due to the furniture. His father taught him about the precision that goes into every piece of work, and how no two jobs are alike. Everyone in the town knew the man and his father, and so the two would be sure to put an incredible amount of care into their work. They wanted to please the people of the town and allow them to make their houses feel more like homes with the help of their furniture.

Rarely, a customer would come back to the shop claiming that there was a defect in their chair or bed frame. This would always bring great shame to the man and his father, and they would be quick to refund the customer and create another piece for them. The pair were not primarily concerned about their reputation in the woodworking business, they wanted the people of the town to be pleased with the furniture that they spent good money on. This method also gave the man and his father more incentive to be extra careful not to make mistakes when crafting their masterpieces, so as not to have to redo them.

The man used this same care as he journeyed through college and began to find interest in the architectural field. This attention to detail allowed him to become successful in the industry very quickly and at a young age. What used to be wood turned into steel and iron, and what were chairs and cabinets became buildings and bridges. It was all the same to the man though, his dream was to build things for others just as his father had shown him. The man wanted to build a family with his wife, but this build was proving more difficult than any he had encountered before. He felt helpless as he watched the fortified life they built come crashing down.

As the rain danced, the man started to search the internet for more alternative methods to having a child. His wife had rejected all the methods he previously identified, as they were not the natural way to have a child. For someone struggling, the internet can be a dangerous place. The man began to read stories of many couples who were also unable to have children. Many of these stories concluded with couples deciding to end their relationship because the pain of trying and failing endlessly was too much to bear. These stories were not new to the man, however, as he had been reading them since the beginning of this ordeal. In the beginning, it was an impossibility that their strong relationship would be brought to a halt for any reason. Slowly, impossibility turned more realistic, and there seemed to be nothing that anyone could do to stop its progression.

It became a daily chore for the man to read these stories and attempt to find a solution online when he knew his search would not be fruitful. After a long day at work, it was all he could do as he walked through the front door to see his wife drowning herself in mindless television. The two did not talk much at all anymore. What used to be vibrant dinner conversations turned into the two of them eating separately, when they did find the rare occasion to eat. The television ran from the early hours in the morning into the late hours of the evening. The man questioned whether his wife was absorbing anything that she was seeing, or if she was just using the noise to drown the sorrows that swam around her mind.

The woman had a job as an interior design specialist before the failures to have a child started to weigh on her. She knew how to look at any room and make it into a place that would be the center of laughter, joy, and love. Her coworkers used to joke that she could have made people feel comfortable in a midnight alleyway. There was always something about a room that she could look at and change for the better, whether it be the paint, drapes, or lighting. It was a pain for everyone around her to see her present room was one covered in gray darkness, lit only by the small dim glare of the television.

It was peculiar that the woman had such a way of bringing people together because she did not come from an encouraging childhood. Her father passed away when she was a young girl, and her mother had to work odd jobs on the streets to make a living for her and her two sisters. The four of them lived in a small downtown apartment that had one window in the corner of the living room. There was one room that was shared by the girls, each of them had a small cot on the floor for sleeping. Food was hard to come by, and luckily neighbors would visit from time to time to help the girls while their mother was out. The apartment was painted eggshell white, and there were only two dainty wooden chairs in the living room. Apart from the chairs, there was only a small wooden table and a stool in the room. After school days, the girls would race home to see who would be able to get to the chairs first, with the loser having the shame of sitting on the small stool.

Despite these conditions, the woman developed the ability to make beautiful creations whenever she was given the opportunity. Many times, she looked over rooms even barer than the one she grew up in and made them into a marvelous display. Her personality was similar. She was able to bring the best out of everyone that she interacted with, no matter what path they had been down in life. She would create love in the hearts of people that did not have anything. This love for creation was the reason that she ended up with the man.

When things started to turn south, the woman began to show a little less cheer when she showed up to work each day. It was immediately noticed by her co-workers, who were very compassionate and apologetic towards the woman for what she was going through. Even the surplus of love surrounding the woman could not save her from the grips of despair as she repeatedly was told she could not have a child. She began to lash out at the people in her workplace, and the customers too. People who used to go out of their way to greet her were now avoiding her, afraid of being on the wrong side of one of her outbursts. Eventually, the store manager had to have a difficult conversation with the woman and asked her to leave until she could bear returning to the job. Now, that was over a year ago, and there was no step closer towards that day arriving.

"Meredith, my parents called earlier and said that they would like to meet us for dinner tomorrow. Should I tell them that you can't attend?" the man spoke over the rain outside as he entered the dungeon like room in which the woman was staring at the television. There were times when the woman seemed that she was somewhat attentive when watching the television, and during those times she would put on children shows. She did this as a cursed reminder of the shows that she would not be able to watch with her child. Today the television was playing a children's show featuring fruits and vegetables. The man was happy when he saw this, firstly because it showed that there was some form of attentiveness going on within his wife's mind, and secondly because he thought that she might answer his question while in this state.

The woman continued to stare at the television as she began to slowly shake her head. The man knew that this would be the answer, he was simply trying to take an opportunity for interaction with his wife. Ever since the last doctor's visit, she had been even more mute than usual. The common procedure after a rejection was for the couple to take a silent ride home and once they returned, try to talk over what they would do next. Common ideas included adding a new exotic herb into the diet or trying to have sex during a different time of the day. They would discuss how they did not trust the last doctor and how they were sure that they would have to find another one for their next visit.

After this last visit, however, the mute ride home evolved into days of silence afterwards. There were no plans on what to do next, not even a droplet from the fountain of optimism. A fountain that the man feared may have sprayed its last beads. With the silence came uncertainty. The man wondered if this meant that there was a big change coming. Would the woman decide to change her mind and go for an alternative solution such as adoption? Would she decide to leave him? Would she wake up in the morning? Would he? The way that this uncertainty developed in the man's brain frightened him. He truly did not know what would come next.

His parents did indeed call him earlier asking if he would be available for dinner. It was routine for them to go out to eat about once per month. These feasts were joyful events before the failures started to pile up. His father and mother were in their seventies, but they lived healthy lives and were still active. They lived 30 minutes away, which made it easy for everyone to meet up for the occasional meal. The man felt grateful to have his parents living nearby, as they were getting up there in age, but when the talks of having a child began it became tiresome. His parents were pushy when it came to wanting a grandchild. Although they remained healthy, they knew that nothing is ever guaranteed, and at their age they saw a waning opportunity to see grandchildren.

When the man and woman first started to fail at having a child, the man's parents were as supportive as everyone else. They would send in new ideas, browsing the internet for the solutions that seemed to keep eluding their son. As the rejections began to pile up, they also began to get frustrated as they saw what was happening to the connection between the man and the woman. They did not understand why the woman was putting herself through such pain when there were other opportunities for her to have a child. Truthfully, that was the same question that many with knowledge of the situation had as well. The woman knew what she wanted, and her unwillingness to bend made the man's parents very upset.

After a few sour dinners, the woman decided that it was for the best if she did not attend any longer. It was evident that the man's parents were not too beaten up about this new development. The dinners started to become more colloquial, cheerful subjects would fly off the walls of the restaurant rather than a dull harping on the elephant in the room. The conversation always seemed to linger, however, in the back of their minds. They knew that it would eventually rear its ugly head and cast a pall over the flowing conversation. The venues would change, but the conversation would always drift in the same direction.

Tonight's venue was Arcane Mill, a small eatery located just down the road from the man's home. The group had never visited the place before. They did enjoy trying out new places around town. At this point, however, it was rare to find a place that they had never heard about or been to.

Drops pattered against the glass window next to the spiral staircase as the man walked upstairs to begin getting ready for dinner. He had always been amused by the idea of the spiral staircase. A structure that could get to great heights without sacrificing much space was a marvel he and his wife could not resist when they were creating their home. The window placed nearby allowed them to look out at the landscape all the way up their ascending journey. Outside was a finely mowed lawn seemingly flat and untouched, the blades of grass perfectly aligned with each other to form a perfectly still sea of green. Beyond that tranquil green sea there stood a line of evergreen trees almost as perfectly placed. With their thick, dark foliage, one could not see through to the neighboring house beyond the trees.

The man entered his room, one that used to be springing with life and energy with the vibrant colors of the sheets, drapes, and pillows. These colors were now strewn across the floor and dulled by the darkness of the room, gathering no brightness from the gray surrounding the house. The woman did not spend too much time in this room anymore, sleeping in front of the television most of the time. She was always the decorator of the room, arranging the pillows so that the room looked to be fit for a king and queen. It was constantly a pleasure to walk in at the end of a long day and feel the structure of a well-made and elegant room. Now though, it was more chore than pleasure. The room can be like the mind of a person. When it is messy and disorganized, it can be quite discomforting.

The man began to put on one of his classic blue button-down shirts and some khaki pants. It was the usual outfit for these dinners with his parents, somewhere between a ballroom dance and a Sunday on the couch. The man was not particularly looking forward to this dinner. The conversation was always brought up soon after he and his wife had just been to the doctor. As the man began to let out a sigh, he noticed the door begin to open out of the corner of his eye. Slowly, the woman peeked her head into the room.

"I think I will join you for dinner this evening."

3

Famine

The ride over to Arcane Mill was a quick but silent one. There was not much traffic on the roads, no one wanting to be out in the pouring rain. The long gray roads stretched further than the eye could see. The woman sat stoically in the passenger seat wearing a navy-blue shirt with jeans. Her gaze sat directed out the window unblinkingly for most of the trip. She had become accustomed to dismissing the man's dinner invitations without a second thought, but tonight was different. Perhaps it was her sickening of the constant patter of the rain hitting their roof, or the lack of food in the kitchen, although she had not been acclimated to eating much lately.

She had not seen the man's parents in quite some time. She remembered the past in which the family would come together as one, and she would feel comfort in those times. It felt to her as if she was getting the family life that she had missed out on when she was a young girl. The conversation, caring for one another's daily routine, and the free-flowing spirit of those pleasant evenings would bring her happiness. It had not been the same since her pregnancy troubles began, but perhaps it was the possibility of rekindling that tarnished flame of family that brought her out this evening. Nonetheless, she did not know what to expect. Surely the man's parents would be surprised to see her. She herself still could not believe she was on the way.

The man, just as shocked, served as the pilot of their chariot into the murky cloud of unknown that the two were riding into. He was a bit too bewildered to turn on the radio in route to the restaurant, and so the rain and the wind provided the entertainment for the voyage. At first, he was thankful that the restaurant was so close to their home, but that turned into scorn as he realized that he would have to prepare more quickly for what was to come. The blinker on the car shone a bright yellow against the rainy gray landscape as it pulled into the desolate parking lot at Arcane Mill. Like a first day matador walking into the arena to face a furred beast, the man exited the family vehicle.

The man's parents, by some stroke of luck, were by the door of the restaurant and noticed the two getting out of the car. The man's father wore a green button down with jeans and some loafers. He was 78 years old with a full, slicked back, white head of hair. He was an able runner back in his day, not so much now but he still was able to move with ease. The man's mother was 73 and sported a long white dress that went with her raven black hair, which was tied up into a ponytail, with some white flip flops. She too had some athletic experience as a gymnast and needed no support at her age. As the two turned, both of their eyes widened when they saw that the woman had joined in on the occasion. They both smiled.

"Hello there Meredith, Joe, nice to see both of you on this beautiful evening," the man's mother said as she stomped in a puddle. She had always been a joker.

"Sarah, Abe, it's great to see the both of you, it has been so long," the woman responded cheerily. For as much buildup as there had been in the car ride over, the event had gotten off to a surprisingly smooth start as the crew exchanged pleasantries and entered the restaurant. As they entered the Arcane Mill, it took the form of a dimly lit dining hall that was filled with wooden tables and chairs. All the tables were the same, a golden brown, well worked and finished, and quite narrow with just two chairs on either side. A few chandeliers hung from the ceiling around the middle of the room, which was not too large itself. The muted yellow bulbs on the chandeliers struggled to overthrow the sea of black that surrounded them. A single rectangle of light flashed from the back of the restaurant before it was swallowed back into the darkness.

There was a scent hanging in the air, one of fresh bread and grapes. Despite the amount of darkness that this place held, the smell gave the impression of eating a freshly cooked meal at a vineyard. There was a slow and steady flow of conversation going around the restaurant, though not many of the wooden seats were occupied. The clatter of forks and knives against porcelain plates overtook this chatter quite easily. The walls of the venue were wooden planks that were a much darker color than the tables. The walls were sparsely decorated, with only a few pictures of the owners and family members who helped run the establishment. The main attraction was hardly visible as it hung against the back wall. It was a large photo of two bears walking through what appeared to be a swamp.

A woman stood at a small wooden podium near the entrance and greeted the group.

"Welcome to Arcane Mill, where the bread is fresh and the wine keeps flowing!" The staff was happy to move two of the tables together to make room for the party. When everyone settled into their seats, another young woman came over and offered a dish of bread. It smelled as if right from the oven, a scent so pleasant that everyone at the table forgot for a moment what else they planned to eat that evening. Time itself was suspended as the soft, smooth butter was glazed across the warm, airy bread.

"Tonight, as a thank you for making it out in this tough weather, we are going to start you all off with a glass of wine on the house!" the waitress gleefully chirped as she began to pass out the menus. The guests nodded in thanks as they remembered that they had not come just for the bread. It was not often that the group would get to drinking at these dinners, but perhaps it would be a good way to loosen them up before the inevitable conversation about the latest visit to the doctor.

The waitress hastily brought over chalices of deep red wine that gently rippled as they were placed in front of the guests. Up until now there had been no mention of the event, and besides the initial shock of seeing the woman arrive, things were flowing effortlessly. The dinner continued similarly as food arrived and more drinks were poured. Ultimately there was a lull, and the clatter of forks, knives, and benign conversation seemed to come to a halt.

"So, what did you figure out at the doctor's office the other day?" The man's father unsheathed the blade from seemingly out of nowhere, "I already have a hunch considering it hasn't been brought up yet." His wife looked him in the face. The man and the woman looked at each other. They all knew that the conversation would be brought up, but did not expect it to be asked like a lightning bolt out of a clear blue sky. The small lights above them seemed to flicker as the group blinked and looked at one another.

"No good news yet but we are starting to think about going to another doctor," the woman replied. She believed she was prepared for this moment.

"Will this one be any different than the other hundred doctors you have visited?" the man's father snapped back quickly. "At this point we would be foolish to think that you two can make us a grandchild. We would have more luck trying to have another child of our own and hoping to see them have children."

There was nothing more that could be said at that point, the blade had struck its target. The man began to get up out of his seat as his chair screeched against the wooden floor. The man's mother gestured her hands towards the man and her husband as if to try and break up a brawl before it began. The woman stared unblinkingly into the soul of the man's father. The man's father looked back at her, his eyes beginning to waver at the sheer force of the look that he was receiving. It was not a look of emotion or hatred; it was a look of death. It made the recipient forget all about the bread and wine. The look made him instantly regret his words.

A sudden tension filled the air in the restaurant as eyes delivered themselves to the unfolding scene. Filled forks halted midair as they prepared to enter gaping mouths. Soon everyone in the restaurant was watching, hoping to see something unusual to interrupt their evening meal. They were not eager that the event advance into tragedy, of course not, but perhaps just a shouting match and maybe a swing or two. No one dared to think of stepping in and assisting if the latter ended up being the case.

For the moment the only sound was the rain hitting against the glass windows of the restaurant. Suddenly, the hard-working chandeliers began to flicker as if notched by the wind from outside. Eyes dashed towards the ceiling as thoughts went from anticipation to worry. Following a moment of flickering, the lights came back on and appeared stable after a few seconds. This diversion seemed to be enough to stop the unfolding charade.

Without a word, the woman stood up from her seat and made her way towards the exit at a deliberate pace. The man and his parents did not utter a word as she left the building, they simply looked at each other with anger and confusion. The chatter around the restaurant began to pick back up as if the event never occurred. Fork ammunition was extinguished and the utensils on their way towards heaping piles of reload.

"Thanks for that Dad," the man broke the silence at the table. "I'm sure Meredith won't be able to contain her excitement when I ask her to dinner again."

"I may have gone a little far there. But you must admit, at this point there is no hope for the two of you to have a child naturally. It has been years of trying and all it has done is destroy your relationship. You know how sensitive of a subject this is for your mother and I. We have been dreaming of having a grandchild for so long." There was pain and remorse in his eyes as he spoke. One could tell that he had been invested in this journey as much as the man and his wife.

The man did not know of the countless hours that his parents had put towards finding a solution for their child. The calls that they made late in the night trying to find a doctor who had success with couples who were struggling to conceive. They wanted to see their son and his wife happy. They also wanted to have the joys of having a grandchild, watching the one that they raised begin to raise another.

"You did go way over the line Abe, but I know that your heart was in the right place," the man's mother commented. "Joe, you know that we want this so badly for you. We also want it for us. Our time to have active lives with our grandchild is running out. This has been a worry of ours ever since your brother –"

The man shot up from the table and began to head out just as the woman had, without a word. This was a conversation that he had heard too many times, one that would not be changed here in the quiet darkness of Arcane Mill. When he exited the restaurant, the woman was standing still staring out into the darkness. Drops of water fell from her, her shirt and jeans had turned soaked black.

The man unlocked the car, "Meredith, I'm sorry for what happened in there. That was unacceptable. I understand if you never want to come to one of these dinners again. Let's get home before it gets too bad out here, it's getting late."

Without a word, the woman entered the vehicle, slowly and deliberately. The ride home was silent except for the window wipers flying across the drenched windshield. All that was visible outside were the streetlights overhead. The two arrived home shortly after, and the car pulled into the garage. The woman spoke.

"I'm going to have to reconsider my place in this family if things don't change."

4

Light

The man and the woman walked swiftly through a pair of automatic double doors into a well-lit lobby. They both sported yellow rain jackets, removing their drop ridden hoods as they walked towards a woman at the front desk. Their boots squeaked steadily against the white tile floor for what seemed like an eternity. It was as if the more steps they took towards the white glass desk, the further away they became. The lobby was filled with wooden chairs that donned blue cushions, all of which were unoccupied. The fluorescent lights on the ceiling floored the space with an overwhelming brightness, contrasting heavily with the darkness from outside. The two atmospheres were set for battle, with the border being the glass windows of the building. This feud went unnoticed though, as the pair strode towards the desk with their eyes directed at the receptionist.

The greeter was a woman with short amber hair and dressed in all white. She flashed a healthy smile as they finally made it to her.

"Glad that you folks could make it here today in this awful weather, what can we do for you?"

"We are the Francis family, here to see Dr. Lucas," the woman responded seemingly excited. It had been a few months since the dinner at Arcane Mill, and things had changed for the better. It was a dark couple of days immediately following, with the man and woman reconsidering the direction of their marriage. After a few days of wandering in the dark void, a ray of light arrived in the form of a letter they received in the mail.

It was a stroke of luck that the letter was not tossed out with the rest of the paper bills. The couple had gotten used to paying their bills online, and most of their invitations were responded to likewise, so they were not accustomed to getting anything of real importance delivered to their mailbox. The daily routine was for the man to go out to the mailbox in the morning, quickly glance at the letters, and then promptly throw them into the trash cans outside of the house. One day during this routine, however, the man caught sight of this peculiar letter.

The letter was in a red envelope, likely the reason why it stood out at first to the man as he shuffled through the bills and offers that would come regularly. It was addressed to Joe and Meredith Francis, and there was a stamp in the corner from the Pear Tree Hospital. The stamp had a tiny version of the hospital on it and included a small golden pear in the upper left corner. This was a peculiar sight to the man because he and the woman had done numerous searches around the area while trying to find a doctor to help them. They made efforts to get to every hospital within a one-hundred-mile radius, and they even extended their search to those doctors that were working outside of the state. Through all this searching, the pair never came across the Pear Tree Hospital.

Considering the dire status of their relationship, the man put his initial speculation aside and tore open the letter right there in the driveway. At first, he speculated that it was a letter asking for a charitable donation. After all, this was likely a startup hospital, being that he had never heard of it before. Not to mention the man had made a name for himself in the architectural industry, and with that name came the money to be able to give to a rising facility such as the hospital.

Quickly, however, this thought was erased when the man saw the card inside the envelope. On the front of it was a stork flying through the clouds and carrying a small child enrobed in a sheet that the stork clasped between its beak. Across the top of the card in cursive red letters read "Rejoice". The inside of the card held only a few sentences:

"Looking for the solution to your issues? Call 601-680-6334 for the answer. We look forward to hearing from you at the Pear Tree Hospital." It was the kind of message that the man would have taken as a cheap trick had the situation been less severe. The stunning absence of information on the card and the spontaneity with which it arrived were generally indicative of a scam.

But there was something puzzling about receiving this letter at this time. How did the sender know about the troubles that the man and woman were having conceiving a child? The man reasoned that he and his wife had been putting their information onto many lists in their search, and perhaps this Pear Tree Hospital had come across this information and decided to reach out. The sender may have known what kind of situation that the man and woman were in, and how desperate they were to find a solution to their problem. Still, the letter was severely lacking information and instruction.

Whatever the case was, the letter drew enough curiosity from the man for him to give the hospital a call later that day. He pondered over the idea of calling for a few hours before deciding that there would be nothing to lose if he dialed the number. He decided not to tell the woman at first because he did not want to give her any false sense of hope with this mysterious invitation. So, the man decided to set himself in his large, cushioned office chair and call whoever had sent this letter.

The phone rang for only half a second. A woman with a welcoming voice answered.

"Pear Tree Hospital, what can we do for you?"

The man explained that he found the letter in his mailbox that morning and he was calling to figure out what was going on.

"Okay Mr. Francis, I will be sending your call over to Dr. Lucas to further explain why you received this letter, please hold," the voice of the hospital responded as soft elevator music began to play in the background of the phone call.

"Hello Mr. Francis, this is Dr. Lucas over at the Pear Tree Hospital. Let me give you some information about myself and explain why you received the letter." The doctor spoke briskly, and with confidence, "I have been working with couples who struggle with childbirth for 15 years now and I was given some of your information from a friend in the field. I am sorry to hear about the troubles that you and your wife have been going through, but I believe I'll be able to help you out. My doctors and I have developed a medicine called Lucidant which has been 100% successful in granting woman natural childbirth after just one dose. You likely haven't heard of it before because we've yet to receive formal approval, but I assure you that there has been no issue with the thousands of women that have tried the product thus far."

The man nearly hung up the phone immediately after hearing this. It sounded like the kind of scam that would come with a scantily worded red envelope in the mail. Yet, there was a faint glimmer of hopefulness in the back of his mind that began to form. What if this doctor was right and this Lucidant could grant him and his wife the child that they longed for so long. The man began to dream of the old life he lived. The smiles with family over warm dinners, the heartfelt summer evenings with his wife out in the backyard, the cheerful greetings he would receive when coming home after a long day of work. The man missed his old life and the simple joys that it brought him, and this doctor was giving him an invitation to return to that life. So, against his trepidation and doubts, the man kept the phone to his ear.

"I know that this must sound like a scam, but the fact that you are still on the line with me shows the value of what I have to offer," the doctor continued as if he had strategically paused after his opening lines, knowing that there would be no immediate response. "I invite you to look me and my team up online, I assure you that we have many happy success stories. Lucidant is a one-time dose and it works for life, many of the families that we have worked with have been blessed with multiple children. So far, the only negative effect of the product is that families need to spend more money on the great times they have with their loved ones!"

The man knew that this deal sounded too good to be true. One pill, which he had never heard of, would be the magic solution to all the problems he encountered over the past years. The doctor even sounded like a scam artist, the way that he perfectly placed his sentences so that he planted an idea in the mind, helping it grow with each additional word. Somehow, this doctor had figured out the man's core issue in life and was saying all the right things to deliver hopes too good to be true. He was wary, but he was desperate.

The seed had been planted, and it was shooting into the sky like a beanstalk to the clouds.

"Thanks for taking the time to speak with me today, Doctor, but this all seems a little too good to be true. We have been searching for hospitals and solutions for over a year and we haven't heard anything about you," the man spoke against his better judgement, knowing that he should have hung up the phone.

"We keep our business here very lowkey, Mr. Francis, as I said we are still working on getting approval of our product but we have no doubts about our facilities. We are privately funded and have an incredible hospital that is not too far a drive from you. This solution is one of our main attractions, and we are still working on getting our name out there so that we can help more families," the Doctor continued as if he knew he had latched onto the desires of his listener.

"Well, I suppose I can talk to my wife about this offer and get back to you. I can't give you any assurances though. I'm very skeptical about what you're telling me right now."

"That is perfectly understandable, my friend. If you are interested, or have any additional questions, you have our number and address. Enjoy the rest of your day," the Doctor replied as he promptly hung up the phone. The man was left standing in his kitchen, questions developing in his mind. He continued to be infatuated with the thoughts of having his wife and family back. This included the wonders they would all encounter with a child in the mix as well. Thoughts of playing catch in the backyard with a child flooded over any doubts that he had about the unknown and uncertain medication the doctor spoke of.

The man stood dumbfounded for a few more moments, still struggling to believe that the phone call had just occurred. He grappled over whether he should tell the woman about what had happened. Surely, she would want to take this medication. She would be willing to do anything to have a child at this point. But this was not a proven medication by any means. Through all the searching that they had done, there was not a trace of this magic fertility pill. There was no telling what kind of hardships this pill could bring with it. The man did not want to bring about the possibility of the woman being hurt by taking this mysterious medication. He remembered that the doctor said there were success stories online and resolved that he would decide on whether to tell the woman after a thorough investigation.

The man at once went to his computer. Internet searches for Lucidant and Dr. Lucas quickly sent him to a page on the Pear Tree Hospital's website. Sure enough, the hospital was located within 30 minutes of the house. The man struggled to conceive how there could have been an unnoticed hospital so close by to the place that he lived at for years. He believed that he knew everything in the reasonable vicinity due to his architectural projects in the area. Normally he would have heard of a building of this size being put up so close to his home.

Just as Dr. Lucas promised, there was a list of success stories on the Lucidant page. The man's computer screen greeted him with the smiling faces of families who were purported to have taken this medication. The pictures of the families were links to their stories about how they struggled to create children and how Lucidant was able to help them instantly. Some families tried fruitlessly for more than a decade, much longer of an ordeal than the man and his wife were going through. The man could not imagine living the way that he had been for as long as a decade.

The website also contained a description of the drug itself: Lucidant is a one-time ingestible pill that has effects that will last for a lifetime. The pill will render a woman fertile, even if her partner has fertility issues. There is no limit to the number of children that may be produced after consumption of Lucidant. The effects of Lucidant do not wither as the woman ages. There are no known negative effects of Lucidant.

The man did not feel any more relieved about the drug now that he had seen it online. He realized that all of this could be an elaborate con used to take advantage of couples who are struggling to conceive. He was likely having the same thoughts that most had before deciding to seek refuge in Lucidant. Lucidant was a last resort, a last opportunity to grasp the fleeting light that eluded the man and his wife for years now. It was a way to mend what was unmendable. Despite the lingering questions about how the drug achieved its purpose, the solution was so bright. Blindingly bright.

Seed

The man and the woman followed the amber haired woman down a long hallway that was well lit by the fluorescent lighting lining the ceiling. The woman walked swiftly as the couple followed, seemingly weighed down by the sogginess of their clothing. They took a left at the end of the hall and the woman let them into a room that was labeled "Dr. Lucas". The two walked in and were greeted by the doctor's smile. He had a wide grin showing teeth as fluorescent as the hallway lights, the gray hairs on his head and sideburns were sharp. He was an older looking man, but still looked as if he could move around a bit.

"Hello again Mr. and Mrs. Francis, it sure is great to see you."

This was not the first time that the two met the doctor. In fact, it had been a good while since the first time they were acquainted. A few days after the man investigated the doctor and his supposed miracle drug, he decided he could no longer wonder about what could be. For all the things that could possibly go wrong, it seemed like the families that were depicted on the website were happy. This pursuit of happiness caused the man to decide he would tell his wife about what he found.

Somewhat surprisingly, the woman did not have much hesitation in the idea after learning about the drug. She had not heard anything of it, and she was not aware that the hospital was so close by either. She said that if there was any chance this was going to allow them to have a child, she was willing to do it. The harm that could be done to her from taking a mysterious and foreign substance was not enough to deter her from the motherhood she so deeply desired. Her eyes began to light up once more with this newfound hope. There comes a time when desperation takes over the thought process completely. The only question she had was when they could go and meet the doctor so that they could begin the process.

This meeting proved to come fairly easily as well. The man called back, and Dr. Lucas was happy to accommodate seeing them on extremely short notice. Within a day they were in the very office that they stood in now. Dr. Lucas was a charming man, and he immediately made the couple feel secure that they were making the correct decision and that they would be joining the ranks of the smiling families on the website soon enough. Any reservation that the two may have had evaporated by the time they left the office after that first meeting. It was as if they were put into a dream-like state, and all the struggling they went through over the previous few years vanished into the mist. They left the office that day with a burning hope that they had not experienced in quite some time.

The doctor promised them that they would be receiving their Lucidant pill in the mail promptly, and he did not lead them astray. Within the week they had the Lucidant pill on their kitchen counter. The pill came in a bright red box just like the letter that originally sent the couple on this journey. Without much hesitation, the man and woman stood eagerly as they ripped open the box and the man poured a glass of water.

The two looked at each other with full eyes, really seeing each other for the first time in ages. The pill, not surprisingly, was red, and it went down very smoothly. That evening the man and woman sat out by a well-lit bonfire in their backyard. There was fall in the air, and they could smell the crispness of the firewood burning against the stone fire pit. Things were almost as they were before this whole ordeal began.

It had been around a month's time since that wind chilled evening in the backyard when the man and woman found their way back into Dr. Lucas's office. He sat in his chair with that grin that appeared to stretch on for miles. His teeth were all aligned and pearly white, the kind of set that would make modest money on any tooth care commercial. The smile was infectious, and the man and woman did not realize that at that moment their faces matched that of the doctor.

"We are ready to take the test and figure out if I have a baby inside of me," the woman rejoiced.

In the weeks since taking the pill the woman became very joyful at first, followed by pangs of sorrow and depression. She was not eating much and struggled with nausea, vomiting, and mood swings. Although she had bouts with these negative emotions, she managed to keep an air of positivity over her throughout. She could tell that something was changing with her body, that she may be carrying precious cargo. It was a feeling she had not felt before, and one that oddly caused her to look forward to her hurling vomiting sessions over the toilet. She fought urges to take a pregnancy test because she wanted to be completely sure of it. She wanted the same doctor who blessed her with the red pill to tell her that she was with child. Thus, the couple found themselves headed to the hospital to see Dr. Lucas on another rain drenched afternoon.

"Please Mrs. Francis, follow my assistant down the hallway where she will administer the test to determine if you're pregnant, though I've got a good feeling I know the answer without the test," Dr. Lucas said as the woman sprung out into the hall, staying a few steps ahead of the young assistant. "Mr. Francis, why don't you wait here with me and we'll discuss some of the next steps." The man stood there in a dream like state, smiling and nodding at the doctor. He could not imagine a world in which this test was going to come back negative, and he was thrilled to be getting his old life back. Not only did he rejoice in the return of some semblance of his old life, but he dreamed again about life raising their child. Visions of kayaking down a luscious river, paddling against the spirals of white crested waters filled his mind as the doctor spoke.

The doctor continued to speak for quite some time, but the man did not listen to a single word. Eventually the woman returned to the room, her face was almost emotionless. There was just a touch of hope in her upturned lip, almost imperceivable. The assistant returned to the room soon after with an envelope that she handed to the doctor. The man and woman simultaneously began to shake with butterflies, their eyes going wide as the moment they had been waiting for finally arrived. Surely, negative news here would mark the end of the loving relationship they had built over the years, but that thought was in neither mind as they awaited the doctor's next words. Heart beats turned to toe taps in a matter of milliseconds, and mouths began to water as they waited for the word of this glorious messenger. The room around the doctor began to turn into a blurred haze and the envelope which the assistant delivered seemed to radiate with energy. The couple fought vigorously to refrain from grasping towards the envelope and ripping it open to reveal its treasure. Their years of struggling failure had led them up to this moment.

"Mrs. Francis, it appears that you are pregnant. Congratulations!" Dr. Lucas proclaimed with the small smile that he presented to so many other couples. Immediately the man and the woman fell into each other's arms and dropped slowly to the floor, tears of thanks filling their faces. All the suffering they went through over the years was released with the flow of water they sent from their eyes. The flow combined to form a river onto the cold tile floors of the office, a river of rejoice. They sobbed harmoniously and it felt as though the room was swaying in a way that rocked the earth gently around the tired souls. The years of failure and misery instantly faded away from their faces, and they were rejuvenated as though they were reborn themselves. Time seemed to float still in the air as the couple continued to hold each other, preparing for their impending new lives.

The doctor sat in the corner of his office, looking out a small window into the rainy abyss. This was a show that he had seen many times, one that he used to feel joy in but now had become almost too regular. Although he did not know the hardships that his patients had gone through before entering his office, he knew that they needed to enjoy their time. Sniffles filled the room and bounced off the white tiles that surrounded it. Tears of joy were a magical thing, especially when combined with the collection of sorrow pouring out of the body.

The couple had not yet looked at each other since hearing the news, but they did not need to. They felt the purity of emotion emanating from their bodies and minds as they celebrated the life that was inside the woman. They both felt as if they had been sinking in a pit of quicksand, with the surface folded well over their eyes. With one last jolt of desperation, they reached their arms into the air in hopes of something to grasp a hold of and pull them out. Their prayers were answered on this rainy day. Finally, there came a moment where the couple locked eyes, followed by an extended embrace. The love that they shared for each other rushed back to the forefront, ready to stand against any darkness that the world could throw at them. The indominable spirit which they once shared aroused from deep within them.

After another minute the couple got up from the ground and proceeded to express their gratitude to the doctor. This was their return to reality, as for many moments they had forgotten where they were in time and place. The tears had not left their faces as they turned to leave the room in which their miracle occurred. The red lines dripped and draped from their eyes to the bottom of their chins. The man turned around and gave one more look of wordless thanks as the couple departed.

The car ride home was silent and even the rain around the car seemed to land more gracefully on its exterior. The roads were clear, and the lights were green as the car's two occupants sat with their lips hesitantly upturned. They had been failing for so long that they did not fully believe what just happened to them. They knew that the test and the results were reality, but still they felt the shadow of a doubt that they may have been dreaming the whole thing up. This doubt was alleviated when the couple got back to their house and looked around at the condition it was in. At once, they began to clean up the sheets and pillows that their depression had strewn across the living room. Once the home was cleaned, the lights turned on, and the television turned off, the couple embraced each other once more.

The two chatted about how thankful they were for the doctor who stumbled into their lives. They reminisced on the harrowing journey they took to get to this point of happiness. Both were sorrowful for the time they spent in depression and anguish, and they felt disappointed in themselves that the situation turned them against their love. There was also a sense of pride in the fact that they both survived the journey, they were successful and going to get all that they ever hoped for. The two felt that after this trial they passed together, there would be no worldly challenge that could shoot them down.

After a while, the two realized that there were others who would be happy to hear the news. The man called his parents and invited them over for a night of celebratory feasting in the backyard. His parents were ecstatic when they heard the news, and they instantly forgot all about the spats and quarrels they had experienced over the past years. Of course, they would be attending dinner in celebration of the future grandchild that they were looking so forward to meeting. The man's father triumphantly declared that he would be making his finest salmon dish, and that his wife would be supplying the wine.

The woman's relationship with her sisters had become distant, as did many of her other relationships. Her mother was living in a nursing home near both of her sisters many miles away. She could not remember the last time she heard their voices, let alone seen them in person. She realized how deeply she missed all of them and the bond that they shared. Together, they survived some of the harshest climates that a big city could bring. She thought about the winter nights where they huddled around the radiator and took turns passing around a loaf of bread. Times were harsh, but they were all together and they were all they needed. Despite all the hardships, they created a happy life together.

The woman went digging through cabinets to try and find her sisters number, eventually finding it tucked away amongst other forgotten trinkets. She looked over the number as her heart began to beat quicker and her palms began to swell. She felt excited that she would be talking to her family after so much time away, but also nervous to discover how they would feel towards her after she neglected their relationship for so long. Her mind went blank as she decided to pick up the phone and dial the number. As the phone began to ring in her ear, she realized she did not know what she would say, and she began to panic. Before she could act, she heard her sister's voice. The woman spoke but it was not heard, as her sister's greeting was simply a pre-recorded message on the answering machine. She decided this would do for now and simply said she needed to talk and to give her a call back.

Later that evening the man's parents showed up with joyous smiles on their faces and they greeted the couple with exceptionally lengthy embraces.

"We're so proud of all the hard work you put into this!" Things resumed as they once were. The group gathered around in the well-lit kitchen and laid down the fish and the wine on the pale marble countertops. It was a kitchen fit for creating a feast, and that is what occurred that evening. The quartet worked in unison, flying around the kitchen narrowly avoiding each other as they leapt through the miniscule lanes they created.

The man's mother oversaw the beverages. She went straight for the celebration glasses on the top shelf. She grabbed four tall goblets and made sure to place them carefully on the countertop. The woman's would be filled with sparkling water, now that she was expecting. She began to chop up fresh tangerines that were grown in bountiful valleys. She paired them with a bowl of washed red grapes. She then popped open a bottle of the finest wine she was able to find at the store, red of course. She was the first to leave the kitchen, going out into the yard to sit by the bonfire and begin the process of lighting it up.

The woman was focused on a delicate garlic bread that she crafted from scratch. The dough was perfectly rolled out on the counter and dressed in flour. She finely chopped the garlic which filled the air with a splendid aroma. She drizzled the dough with oil as she set the oven. Lastly, she sprinkled some parmesan cheese onto the top of the dough as she gracefully placed it into the oven and retreated from the kitchen to join the man's mother outside and help her to light up the evening.

The man started the stove up and was creating a sauce for the salmon. He deftly diced up an onion, hardly having the tears left in him to cry. Next came some of the garlic that the woman chopped, and some spinach which was quickly washed in the sink. All that was left was heavy whipping cream and a cup of white wine to add to the skillet. Once the ingredients were on the stove, the man looked to his father before departing to join the others outside.

The man's father was the last one remaining. He skillfully seasoned the large piece of salmon. He felt the tender fish under his hands as he massaged a mixture of garlic, cumin, and chili powder into the pink flesh. He put the salmon in the oven and then waited, watching the others outside with a wide smile on his face. When the fish was done cooking, he brought it out and drenched it in the sauce. In two trips, he brought the feast out to his family.

The family sat and laughed out by the fire as they had done so many nights in the past. They picked up right where they left off. It was as if all the fighting and the hard times between the group evaporated. Toasts were made and they even broke out into a cheer about how they would need to thank the wonderful doctor who made this miracle occur. All the while, the fire raged and lit up the evening as it began to slowly darken.

At a point where the conversation of the evening stalled, the group collectively looked out into the beautiful backyard. The grass was freshly mowed up until the outskirts of the yard where it reached the tree line. The trees stood tall, perfectly symmetrical and with a beautiful deep green hue. It was clear at first sight that these trees had been standing for many years. It was as if they mastered their craft, standing in complete harmony but gracefully bowing to the occasional wind. The crickets were chirping in the forest's interior, their sounds a constant reminder that there was bountiful life within the woodland trees. The noises of the crickets were joined by the crackle of the bonfire, creating an atmosphere in which it was impossible to think of anything except the still movements of the world.

It became a cool evening. There were even a few fireflies dancing in the night sky. Their flickering orange glow sporadically appeared with the dark blue sky as a background, creating a childlike anticipation of where the next spark would radiate. The family peered with joy into the night sky and realized eventually that they had not been thinking but instead observing. One of the most difficult things to do is to think of nothing, right when the mind realizes that it has wandered into nothingness, the thoughts return. They instantly began to think about how thankful they were to be in this position. Their family would be growing soon, and they overcame so much to get to this point. Son or daughter, the child would be loved.

As the evening began to wind down, the family prepared for the departure of the man's parents into the night. Emotions ran high during a tear-filled goodbye at the front door. It was not sadness that struck the family as they parted, it was overwhelming emotion for what was to come. The man and woman finally got their wish, but they knew not what kinds of troubles would come with being parents. The man's mother and father knew this path well, but they too were venturing into the unclaimed territory of grandparenthood. There were joyful promises to keep returning to their weekly meetings, and each of them thought of the fun times they were all going to enjoy together as a family once again.

The man's parents left. Slowly, the house began to shut down. Lights turned off, appliances the same, drapes shut. The man and woman began to ascend the spiral staircase together. For the first time in many nights, they would share their bed together this evening. As the two retreated under the covers and turned out the lights, they looked to each other and smiled. They had overcome the long and difficult journey. Although at times they drifted apart, they were now together and happy.

It was around two in the morning when the man suddenly woke up from what had been a very pleasant sleep next to his wife. He was not sweating, and he could not remember any dream which would have woken him in such a flash. In fact, it was one of those times where reality, the evening that the family just enjoyed, felt like a dream. The man sat up and began to rub his eyes, wondering how much more time he would have to sleep before he needed to get to work for the day. In the corner of the room, just visible, there was a window looking down into the backyard. A light drizzle tapped on the window as if it were the culprit who woke the man from his deep slumber. The man looked closer out into the yard as his eyebrows turned downward in focus and confusion. The firepit was there, roaring into the night as if it were never quenched.

The man remembered that they turned everything off before ascending to their sleep, so he was confused as to what was going on. Slowly, he turned his legs out from under the covers and began the torturous process of getting out of bed at two in the morning. As he walked down the spiral staircase, he wondered whether it was something in the wires that had lit the fire pit once more. He was very skilled with the mechanics of things. Surely, he would be able to figure out some scientific explanation for the issue another time.

He slid open the glass back door so that he could enter the yard and turn off the fire. Instantly he shuddered, in the wee hours of the night the air was overcome by frost. The pleasant cool of the early evening turned into a shivering cold by the dark of midnight. The man's teeth chattered as he slowly made his way towards the fire, which was not doing much to warm him. He could hardly open his eyes when he reached the pit and began to bend down to turn the knob off. He heard the click of the knob into the off position, but it was overpowered by a scuffle of leaves that came from behind him. It was only then that the man realized the world had gone quiet, no longer were the crickets chirping nor the fireflies sparking up in the night. A stillness hung in the air like a fishing hook drifting amidst the deep calm of the ocean.

The man turned around and was instantly thrown into a trance. Goosebumps and hairs stood up all over his body and he instantly dropped a bead of sweat down his forehead. His mouth dropped and his jaw hung suspended in the cold air. He felt a shockwave go through his body, feeling like pins and needles stacking on top of each other from the soles of his feet to the top of his crown. His spirit dropped well into his stomach, he tried to let out a curdling scream, but no sound would come out of his mouth. He felt as if his whole body was being lifted into the air, yet the soles of his feet remained on the ground. The eyes that he was looking into were not from this world.

Staring back at the man, standing in the grass of the backyard, was a tall pale figure with long eyes as dark as coal. It had what appeared to be a gaping mouth, and teeth that were almost the size of the man's skull. The figure did not have any ears nor nose, but instead slits that cut through the side of its large head. The creature had long wispy white hair that dragged itself across the figure's gaunt shoulders in the wind. The creature stood high, almost double the height of the man, on a long and thin torso that was as white as the bright side of the moon. Its hands were tipped with fingers that seemed to be as long as broomsticks, almost stretching down to the ground beneath the beast. Its feet, equally daunting, were planted deep into the grass of the backyard. The moon glimmered against the creature's back as it calmly looked into the eyes of the shocked man in front of it. The stillness of the night whispered around the two figures standing in the backyard.

The man stood still without the ability to speak or move. His mind raced with thoughts of how he would be able to wake up from this nightmare. As his thoughts continued, his heart felt as if it were about to explode from his chest. The creature began to move forward its right arm. Its hand rose in a steady drift through the air, with the long fingers slowly stalking behind the white hand. Once the hand was pointed towards the man, a finger extended until it was close enough for the man to reach out and grasp it. The creature's mouth did not move, but the man began to hear a voice in his head. It was a raspy, slow, drawn-out voice that was something of horror in its own right.

"You will have a son, but he will not live the life that you will hope for him. He will be led down a path in life that will result in great harm to many. No matter what you do, your son will be a vicious ruler who causes the deaths of many. He will cause pain, suffering, and tragedy that will change the course of this world forever. Only you have the power to make this right, terminate this pregnancy no matter the cost. Whatever that cost may be, it will be nothing compared to the countless lives that would be saved. It is up to you to make this decision. Choose wisely."

The rasping voice left the man's head as he began to feel his body settling back into the earth below him. He could not comprehend what he had just heard, still staring in shock at the creature that stood before him. For a brief moment it appeared that a star was streaking by, far above the tips of the green trees. Almost immediately, the man's eyes closed, and he fell to the ground, his body like a limp rag.

Rise

The morning sunlight peeked through the curtains as the man and woman slowly opened their eyes to a new day. They were early risers, not able to keep their minds silent as the world awoke around them. Their hardwood floor began to light up with the sun's rays as they looked at each other. Their eyes met and lit up with happiness as they soaked in the aftermath of what had been a jubilant day. Awakening next to one another to start the new day was confirmation that the whole day prior, and all of the joy that came with it, had been real. The two soaked each other in for a while before they decided it was time to get up and start preparing for work.

Like clockwork, they delved back into routines of old. Stumbling to the drawers, getting dressed for the day, sliding past each other in the bathroom as they brushed their teeth and put on ointments. All the while, there were smiles on their faces and sweet tunes running through their heads. Earrings and watches were put on, hair was brushed, and shoes were laced. They were silently amazed at how fast their home had returned to them.

The woman decided that she would be going back to her workplace on this day. She had not been to her interior design job in quite some time, but she built up a lot of good will there over the years. When she was asked to leave by her boss, he assured her that there would be a spot waiting for her when she felt able to return. She had not left on unrepairable terms with anyone, and most of the group knew that she was going through unbearable times.

It was not until this morning that the woman realized how much she missed her job. She found great satisfaction in helping customers who were looking to create their homes and turn them into a place fit for a family. The woman was blessed with the eye for a pleasant household, and she wanted once again to share that talent with her customers. She was the first to get down to the kitchen, making herself an espresso to begin the day. The sweet taste of espresso and the rays of morning sunshine coming in from the backyard made for a beautiful atmosphere. The woman breathed deeply, taking in the moment and feeling confident about the day. She met the man at the front door, and the two shared a kiss before she departed for a hard day's work.

The man was headed in the other direction, on his way towards the kitchen. It was a slow-moving morning for him. His success in the architectural field had given him quite a bit of leeway with his schedule. Most of the time, he could be found out in the world looking for plots of land to develop for future projects. Periodically, he would stumble upon a fortunate soul who needed the eyes of an expert to get their business up and running. Most good businesses start with an idea, but many times that idea cannot be carried out without a physical space, a building, to host the creative minds in developing their plan.

When he was not out looking for land or clients, the man did have a small office that he continued to run in the city. He had a loyal team there, a secretary and two apprentices whom he had been training for many years. They were always

excited to see him when he strolled into the office, usually
bearing some sort of reward for his team. Whenever the man
came around, they knew there was something new that he
would be willing to teach them about architecture, or simply
about life in general.

The man got to the kitchen and began his morning
routine, starting up a fresh pot of coffee and heating up the
stove to prepare some eggs. There was something about this
morning that made the man feel he had no worries in the world.
He smiled widely as he flipped his eggs up from the pan into
the air. The coffee had a delicious taste to it, he felt as if it were
the first time he sipped the stimulant. The grin remained on the
man's face as he took his gaze to the sunlight coming in from
the backyard. Outside was a sun shower that was tapping
gently against the glass.

The man instantly shuddered, and he felt a familiar cold
jolt of lightning running through his body. He dropped his fork
full of eggs down onto the counter, the metal clattering against
the stone, and the eggs being further scrambled. Up until he
looked to the backyard, he had no recollection of what
happened early that morning. Now, it was as if a dam collapsed
within his mind, and it was now overflowing with thought. His

memory flooded with the vision of the creature he had seen in the backyard. In his mind, he found himself staring into those dark eyes that seemed only to be a view into an empty endless space. The slow drawl of the creature's voice in the back of his mind made the hairs on his neck point skyward. Sweat started to drip down the sides of his cheek as the chill in his body continued.

Now that the man was remembering the visions, he thought it must have been a terrible nightmare. As he picked his fork back up, he tried to clear his mind of the creature and forget it for good. The thoughts kept tugging at his mind. All of what he experienced in the yard felt so real. The chill in his bones, the silence of the cool black night, and the rigidity he felt throughout his body while he was listening to what the beast had to say. The words of the speech were seared into the man's mind. The man sat and stared at his kitchen cabinets while he searched his mind for reasons why this event could not have been true.

What was this creature and why had it come to him? How would it know anything about the child that the man and woman just found out they would be having? Why had he awakened in his bedroom as if nothing happened? The last thing that the man could remember was not being able to move his body and falling sharply to the ground after seeing a swift flash in the sky. He did not feel any pain when he hit the ground, just heard the thud of his body against the cold backyard porch. For a day that felt like a dream, it was a cruel joke that it had to end with a nightmare.

It began to rain harder outside as the sun faded away behind clouds of gray. A slight fog began to settle over the trees in the yard. The man decided that he would go out into the yard and investigate the area. He opened the doors to the backyard, still in his morning lounging gear of a t-shirt and shorts. Immediately his clothes were soaked by the rain which was pouring down by now. Rain dripped off the tip of his nose, but he could not feel it, nor did he care. He looked down at the area near the fire pit where he had fallen. There were no signs of any fall, no change in the furniture around the pit.

He then looked over to the grass where he remembered the beast standing tall. The creature looked to be heavy and large, and surely it would have left footprints in the soft grass of the yard. To the man's surprise, there was also nothing to be seen in the grass nor in the rest of the yard, which he very carefully scoped. He assured himself that perhaps the incident was a dream after all. Still, it was nothing like any other dream he had ever experienced. Most dreams he would have forgotten soon after waking, but this was one that jolted back into his memory as fast as a jackrabbit escaping an angry farmer. Despite the evidence to the contrary, he could not be sure that what he saw was not real.

He decided that he would try to take his mind off the event by getting into some work for the day. He enjoyed the freedom and flexibility that came with his architectural position, being able to work from the comforts of home, on the road, and in his town office space. People he worked with never could expect him to be in a certain place at a specific time, but he would always remain available on his cell phone. Although face-to-face meetings with his staff were lessened, he had an increased ability to be more productive in the field. Instead of idling at his office, he would be able to go out in search of prospective clients in need of his insight and creativity.

The man sat quietly in his soft leather chair and began to go through his morning routine to start out the day. Although his mind was wandering, he could not help but bathe in the joy that the prior day had brought him. He thought about this as he began a morning call with his coworkers who were all situated at the town office. It was a small team of people coming from diverse backgrounds. There was Sam, who graduated at the top of her class from a large university on the west coast. She specialized in communication and would make sure that the man and his clients were on the same page. David, who started off in a small town in the Midwest, got his name on the map when he helped create the largest space station in the country. He was primarily focused on helping the man acquire clients. Finally, there was Rachel, an older woman who worked to keep the office up and running. She did everything from taking office phone calls to making sure the group was able to meet regularly.

The group was thrilled to hear that the man was finally going to be having the child he desired for so long. They were a tight-knit office, knowing more about one another than other offices generally would. The group truly cared for one another, and they were all genuinely happy to hear about the positivity in the lives of their colleagues. Although the man was their employer and boss, the group looked to him as a friend with whom they could share anything. After receiving congratulations, the man began to inform the team on a job he had his eyes on.

A few months ago, the man had been driving around the local area looking for potential clients when he stumbled upon a dirt path leading into open plains. It was whenever the man drove by these open plains by his house that he thought of the possibilities the land held for buildings. He always thought that if someone would come to him with an idea for a development there, he would build it without hesitation. The land was not far from the residential neighborhoods, and it was close enough to the city that it could one day be seen as a rural extension of the city's happenings. It was a prime spot for people who were looking to find some entertainment on the outskirts of town, not looking to get into the busy city in order to find it.

As the man drove by the path, he noticed that there were tire marks peeling off from the road and traveling into the grassy knoll. He drove a few seconds further down the road before veering his car around and deciding to begin driving down the path the investigate. If someone was out in the field looking to build, the man wanted to be the first to offer his services. This adventure took him a few minutes of driving down the dirt path, which gradually turned into tall grass. Eventually one could look all around and the only thing they would see was the high grass rising around the moving vehicle. Finally, the man arrived at a bit of a clearing.

There was another man standing there, he was tall and wore a jean suit and a tan cowboy hat. He stood there looking out into the grassy distance, seeming to not even notice that another car had arrived at the scene. The man slowly pulled up his car next to the other car parked in the grass, a large gray truck. When he swung open his door, the man in the jean suit quickly looked towards him.

"Howdy there fella," he said with a deep southern accent and a grin, "what seems to have brought you out here to these hallowed grounds?"

"I stumbled upon your tracks leading out here into the fields. I was wondering what it was you're doing out here. I'm an architect, been hoping someone would come along to this land for some time. There's something about this place that makes me want to build, a feeling that there could be great success with a collection of buildings placed here," the man responded. There was something friendly and inviting about this man in the jean suit. He seemed to be a person who knew about the power of money and how to make it.

"Well, you may have stumbled upon the right man. Name's Bernard," the man in the jean suit declared, still smiling wide. "I've had my eyes on this spot since I moved into town a few months ago. Endless fields here, plenty of room to build and right by the city as well. Yes… I've often dreamed of finding a place like this to make my ideas into reality." The man could see the vision, enthusiasm, and drive emanating from Bernard's eyes as he continued to look out into the open field.

The man had acquired a sense of knowing when someone had the belief that they were on the verge of something great, and this Bernard seemed to be confident in whatever he was planning. One issue that the man ran into often, however, was that people could often be tricked into believing their foolish ideas were solid gold. He had long prior resolved to always ensure the legitimacy of an idea before offering his support.

"I like to hear that kind of inspiration," the man said curiously, wondering what Bernard had in mind for the location. "I do think that the people around here could benefit from more entertainment. I see people in the neighborhoods and in the city that are working hard constantly. Day after day, they struggle through the busy lives that they've built for themselves. Most of the people work throughout the day, only to return to their homes worn down from all the energy they've expended. Part of why I build is to bring people more joy in the way they spend their recreational lives. If people aren't enjoying what they're doing in their lives, then I feel poorly for them and wish to help."

Bernard responded, "I agree with you there my friend. I have noticed the drought on entertainment since I came to this land. Where I come from, that is something you would never see. I come from a place where work and play are intertwined, where all the townspeople would get their work done as they celebrated living. When someone had enough of the day's work, they could find themselves already present in an area where they could enjoy the entertainment. In other words, work and entertainment were one in the same. I haven't seen that in this city. Respectfully, what I see is a lifeless gray jungle which percolates with no freedom. I see people moving through their lives, but they are not living. Work is how we evolve as a society, but what is it all worth if we cannot enjoy the time that we have here? What is your name by the way, pal?"

"Joe Francis," the man said as he extended his hand. Bernard grabbed it and gave it a hearty shake. The man was enjoying what he was hearing from Bernard. He could sense the ambition in Bernard, and that he too was a person who wanted to help those around him. Sure, the man himself had at times felt as if he was simply spinning the tires throughout his life. Although he did love his job and the leeway that it gave him, he could not help but worry for those who were not as fortunate as himself. All the people who showed up to that gray jungle every day just to get by, to keep up with their bills and support their families. It was a noble thing to do, to go through the struggle day after day. "Tell me a bit more about this entertaining land that you come from."

Bernard began to tell the man, "As I said, it was a place where people lived free, and all the good things in life were within their palms. Of course, I believe in hard work and that everyone should put in their share of effort to keep the world spinning, but none of that is any good if that hard work isn't relieved through entertainment. The way it was back there, people would work harder and more efficiently because they loved their jobs and the joy that they were bringing to others. What good is it living on this huge rock if we can't enjoy the time that we spend on it?"

"And what kind of work were these people affiliated with?"

"All the things that bring the simple man joy after a hard day's work. Bars for socializing, gambling halls for those with a taste for risk, and gentlemen's clubs for those who need a rejuvenated spirit," Bernard replied. "The kinds of things that other towns in this world would tuck away hidden in shame, this old town would broadcast proudly. The facilities were well integrated into the surrounding community, and the whole ecosystem benefited because of it. Crime went down, people went home happy in the evenings, and money kept coming in by the boatload."

"It's hard to see how crimes were down and families happy in a place like that, those vices lead to violence and destroy families," the man recoiled as he began to revise his view of this entrepreneur. The man thought of the surrounding community in his town, full of industrious families with young children. The nearby city may not have had everything, but it did have some of the best school systems in the region, and a bevy of family friendly events to choose from. There were even talks of bringing a professional basketball team into the city. What kind of impact would it have on the surrounding community if this nearby land was used for the activities that Bernard was promoting? The way he told it, there would be no secret what was going on out in the fields so close to the precious schools and homes that made the community what it was.

"That's what they always say, but I tell you, when there's money coming in, the problems tend to look the other way. There's always a solution when moon-sized truckloads of green are coming in. The way this land is situated, so close to the city and the neighborhoods, I know I would make a fortune here in a few short years. Way I see it, it's off the path enough for those who don't want to be associated, and close enough for those that do. I've seen a small town turned into a metropolis in a matter of months after going to systems similar to the one I propose. All I need to start up with is one central hub, a building that can serve as the nucleus to my plans."

If Bernard was telling the truth, the man thought, this could be a huge opportunity for him to build. Of course, this was the area that the man long dreamed of building on, and he had been on the lookout for a massive opportunity such as this for quite some time. If an idea like this were to hit, he may be world renowned in the architectural business. His works could stand for generations, being remembered forever. Surely though, he had seen plans like this fail many times, it was always seen as taboo to drink, gamble, and solicit sex. These were not the types of establishments that would support wholesome family activity. How would these buildings and this town be remembered? Still, however, the idea of a metropolis rising up from these grounds tugged at the man.

"What do you want to call this place?"

"Sadie and Gunther's," Bernard smiled, "named after two of the finest dogs you would ever meet. They soaked in the joy of each fleeting moment; you could see it in their eyes. Happy lives they lived, long lasting too. They weren't able to make the journey to these parts with me, but I'll always remember them and the times well spent." With that Bernard tipped his hat, turned away from the man, and began walking out into the open field ahead of them. The man took one last look at Bernard in the middle of the field and then turned towards his car. As he drove out of the field, he thought of the creation he could choose to make.

Now, back in his home office talking to his team, the
man recounted his meeting with Bernard and said that he was
seriously considering the idea he had been presented with. The
team seemed reserved about the idea, but they also seemed to
acknowledge that with the riches Bernard promised, they
would be able to retire early. There were four of them, but the
decision would clearly have to be made by the man on whether
to pursue the opportunity.

The man was pondering the build when he saw a flash
of the creature he had seen the night before. The creature talked
about the man's future son becoming a person who created
great terror in the lives of others. The man was amazed at how
vividly he could still remember these visions. His mind
wandered. What kind of person would he be if he helped to
create these kinds of establishments in the town so close to
where his child would grow up. Bars, casinos, and strip clubs,
clearly every kid in town would become aware that these
places were so close to their homes. When the man was
younger, the idea of going to these kinds of businesses was
often a taboo topic of discussion with his friends. What kinds
of things would the children of the town learn if they were to
so easily be able to frequent such places? Would this decision

be the one that would send his son down the path of destruction?

The man shook his head as if snapping out of a haze. He let his team know that he would be doing some more research and thinking over their next move. He wondered why he was letting a dream affect his decision making about critical business decisions he needed to make. Would he live on questioning his every move to avoid playing his part in molding the child that the beast warned him of? He decided that he would have to clear his mind and his calendar for the rest of the morning.

It was times like this where the man was most grateful for his job flexibility. He would often be able to go on bike rides to collect his thoughts during long and stressful days. A vibrant green road bike sat in his garage waiting to serve its duty. The bike was in great condition, given the fact that it was a few years old at this point. The man would always make a point of cleaning off his bike, even down to the gears, whenever he came back from a ride. This green bike helped the man get over many difficult situations in his life. It had been seeing increased action in recent years.

Some days he would ride around the block, others he would ride miles on end as far as his legs would go. This was one of those days where the man felt he would need an extra-long ride to help unravel the circus occurring in his mind. He started out towards those fields where he met with Bernard. It was a rainy day, but the downpour was not overwhelming. The drops of rain bounced against the man's red helmet which he always made sure to wear. Small streams of water trickled down the slope of the helmet and bounced gracefully onto the pavement below the moving bike. The clouds stood nearly still and gray overhead, floating into the distance as far as the eye could see.

Visions of the beast briefly flashed into the man's mind as he tried to maintain his attention and keep his eyes focused on the road. Thoughts trickled in about the decision he would have to make. What if the encounter with the creature was real, and its words truthful? He thought of all the joy that he shared with his family the night before, and what they would think if he told them about his visions. Likely, they would call him crazy and say that he was just having anxiety related to the pressures of becoming a father. Clearly, the road to being a father is not one that you can learn much about if you are not taking the steps down the path yourself. Seldom does one hear from a couple saying that they regret their decision to have a child. To the man, the night prior served as a hope for how simple his life would be now that he was going to be a father.

And what if it was true that he would raise a son who would turn out to be a horror to the lives of many? The man grimaced as he thought about the many dictators that he had learned and heard about throughout the years. All of them had come from far off lands which he had never ventured to, but their stories were so gruesome that they made it to the man's modest town. He knew not what drove these men to the point of devastating entire races of people and destroying generations of families. He questioned how he would raise a son to be this way if he did not have that kind of hate inside him. But what of that warning? Would his child be destined to have a treacherous heart, regardless of how the man raised him?

The bike's wheels continued to spin at a rapid pace as they moved further down the road which seemed to stretch on forever. The pavement beneath them was well paved, there was nary a bump nor wobble in their consistent flow. The wheels moved as time does, a lasting and unstoppable drift. One of the few absolutes in life is that time will continue as the world around us changes, grows, and eventually returns to the earth from which it came, all things bowing to time.

And what of the woman's fate if the man were to tell her of what he saw. Would he damn her to know the same script in which her child would grow up to be evil? She was already back at work and enjoying her life as a future mother, how could the man bear to send her spiraling back into the depression that she suffered through for the past years? These thoughts spun through the man's head as quickly as the wheels of his bike.

What would be the solution anyway if this were the case, the man thought. He was against the idea of abortion, but would it be a different tale if the life being aborted was going to cause so much harm to the world? The beast had not told him the means to the end, just the result, and that would be pain and terror to all. At the same time, the man thought about the horror he would see in his family's eyes if he were to suggest aborting the child that they tried for so long to conceive.

At this point the road came to a fork, splitting into two divergent paths. The rain continued to come down, quickening in pace. Puddles formed under the bike's tires, and small waves splashed as the biker cut through them. The rider was not sure which route he would take as the road split paths. It was not until the last second that he chose, and the madman rode onward into the delusions of the road.

Shrink

The night was dark and the rain outside of the house was gruesome. It pounded against the roof of the house like soldiers marching. The man sat at his kitchen counter looking out into the backyard. There was a wall of rain blocking his vision, so he could hardly make out the fire pit. He sat thinking and waiting for his wife to return from her first day back at work. In the past, he would always be waiting for her when she returned after a long day. He would greet her with a smile and a warm meal. She never had to worry about what to eat after work.

After what felt like decades, the woman finally came through the front door soaked yet wearing a beaming smile.

She gracefully put down her bags and went into the kitchen. To her delight, she saw the man sitting there waiting for her, just like the old days. She gave him a kiss and they started to talk about their days.

The woman had a smooth transition back into her workplace, to the surprise of none. She was the first to arrive at the store in the morning, and she made sure to greet her coworkers warmly when they came in still tired out from the weekend. Her coworkers were shocked to see her only for a moment, before they were reminded of how lovely it was to have the woman working in the store with them. Whenever she was around, customers would find their way to her, even if they had no business buying what she was offering. Coworkers would take their lunches over to her workstation so they could converse and listen to the woman work her magic on the customers. A customer could head into the store not intending to spend a dime and leave it spending hundreds on the woman's services, but they did not mind at all.

The man and woman chatted as though there were not a problem in the world. To both, it was amazing how quickly they were able to rekindle the flame that burned so brightly between them for so long. Anyone could see the deep joy and love for life that returned to the deep brown eyes of the woman. The man was taken captive by the stories she told him of what she encountered that day, just simple tasks really, but the way she spoke of them was encaptivating. After falling back down to earth, the two looked into each other's eyes happily and thought of how thankful they were that things were back to normal.

Silently, thoughts began to creep into the man's mind about how he would do anything to keep this feeling of joy with his wife alive. He wondered what would happen if he told her that she was perhaps carrying a mass murderer inside of her. The joy in her eyes would turn upside down immediately, she would call him insane, and their wonderful evening would be ruined. The man cursed his own mind for thieving the joy of this moment away. It was a time in which the couple should have been celebrating without reservation, but the man's visions kept him from fully appreciating what he had.

His mind persisted. Was the thing that he saw meant to be some kind of religious warning? He had heard tales of divine creatures coming to mortals to tell them prophecies of the future. The man was not very religious, but he did have a belief that there was something else out there watching. With a universe so vast, there was no chance that the whole cosmos had occurred from coincidence. Would he decide to pursue his own happiness, and that of his family, or would he choose to do something for the greater good of the world?

The man blinked and his focus returned to the woman who had resumed chatting about what she did throughout the day. Suddenly, the phone began to ring from the corner of the kitchen. The woman stopped talking on a dime as her eyes darted cautiously over to the phone. She remembered the message she had left for her sister the day before. Nerves gripped her as she prepared for what could be her sister on the other line, tensions stemming from having not spoken to her in so long. Neither of the two moved as the phone continued to ring and finally the answering machine picked up. A woman's voice played on the machine, "Please take the time to come vote to elect Mia Falcon for mayor next week, the ideas she has for this town will have us all soaring with joy!"

The woman took a deep breath and returned her eyes to the man. She noticed that his gaze had shifted to the backyard, and he looked a bit worried. It was then that she realized there was no dinner prepared for her, a classic staple of her old life. Perhaps, she thought, things had not slipped so perfectly back into their old ways. She assured herself that everything would get back to normal shortly, it had been so long that the couple struggled. She began to make her way upstairs to decompress after a long and exciting day of work.

It took a few moments for the man to look back into the kitchen and realize that the woman had left. After a few more seconds of thought, he headed over to his office and sat down in his leather chair. He began to search the internet for therapists in the area. He felt that he would need to talk about what he had seen with an unbiased party.

The man had never been one for therapy. In the past, he could freely share all his troubles with the woman. They would talk for hours about the issues in each other's lives. They would listen deeply and with care before offering their best advice. In more recent times, that avenue of relief was not available due to the disconnect in their communication. They tried to go to therapy a few times when their relationship began to break down, but they were never able to gain much ground. It was as if they were going to therapy to try and rediscover something they had in the past, rather than working towards a better relationship in the future. Short answers and unwillingness to talk resulted in an unpleasant experience for both.

Now the man was dying to get someone else's opinion on what he saw. Surely, a therapist would have run into patients with dreams such as this before. A good therapist may be able to explain to the man why he saw what he did, and what it may mean for him. The man heard of people who dreamt due to uncertainty in their lives. Usually, the more vivid the dream, the stronger the feeling. He felt that he had already devoted too much thought to the matter alone, and wanted to find out what another could take from the situation.

The man was quickly able to find a therapist who worked in the town near his office. Within a week he was walking through the front doors. He found himself in a dimly lit room as drops of water from the rain outside began to descend on his yellow rain jacket. The room had a cozy feel to it. There were only a few chairs in the room, they had soft plush leather, and they were spread apart so that clients could have a sense of independence before heading back to see the therapist. There was not much light in the room, just a couple of tall lamps in the corners that provided enough light for guests to complete their registration forms. There was soft

Etruscan music playing on a small speaker in the corner, soothing music for those who were waiting to enter a place of thought.

On the walls were many fine paintings. One which stood out to the man was The Feast of Venus by Rubens. He looked around and noticed that there were sculptures of ancient philosophers such as Socrates and Aristotle. There was something about being in the room that invited the man into quiet contemplation. He took his seat next to the cold head of Aristotle as he began to wait patiently for his name to be called. There was an older woman behind the receptionist's perch, with flowing dark hair and a smile on her face. Her skin was pale as a stone pillar, and she had a very inviting aura about her. Eventually she called out, "Mr. Francis, we are ready for you!"

The man rose slowly and followed the woman down the comfortable halls of the building which were lined with more ancient art. She led him into a room and closed the door behind him with that inviting smile still lingering on her face. The man took a step inside where he was greeted by a man in a regal leather chair.

"Thank you for coming in Mr. Francis, my name is Marcus Andrews, and I am glad that you have come to see me today." Marcus was a confident looking man who had flowing dark curly hair and a beard to match it. He sat tall yet relaxed in his elegant chair which seemed to be fit for a king. His cool eyes gazed into the man's and invited him to speak without Marcus having to say a word.

"Hey Marcus, I'm Joe, I am equally grateful that you're willing to hear me out today," the man responded.

"My pleasure, Joe," Marcus replied in a friendly tone. "I have had the pleasure of becoming acquainted with your work, I have been very impressed with your buildings around this town. Believe it or not, the construction of my home was based off homes that you helped design in the area. I was thrilled when I heard that you would be coming in to speak with me today."

"I'm happy to hear that, and I hope that the home has served you well Marcus. I'm proud of the impact that I've made on this city and the people around it. It's always great to hear from those whom I have had an influence on. Unfortunately, I didn't come here today to discuss my latest ideas for architecture. I sought you out today because I have become troubled by some recent visions."

"As is often the case," said Marcus curiously. "Please Joe, tell me what troubles you."

"Well, my wife and I for a long time were attempting to conceive a child, but to no avail. We tried everything, different medications, doctors, methods, but we couldn't solve the issue, and it was tearing us apart. Finally, we stumbled upon this doctor, Lucas, who was able to give us the answers to all our problems. He was our last resort, and he put us onto this experimental pill that his company had been successfully using on other couples. We tried it out and within a few weeks, we were in his office and he was telling us that my wife was pregnant. We cried tears of joy that day, and the whole day was a celebration with my parents and my wife. It all truly felt like a dream. Then, that evening, I had this vision."

"First off, congratulations to you and your wife. I was lucky enough to have many children, I can't imagine how difficult it was for you and your wife to struggle to have one. It sounds like there were a lot of vibrant emotions for the both of you on that day of celebration. You must have felt love from your family and the surroundings. Now tell me, what did you see?"

"I awoke in the middle of the night, well I'm not sure if I was awake or dreaming, and I noticed that there was light coming from the backyard. I made my way out back and instantly felt a chill in the air. Behind me was some sort of thing – a beast is the best way that I can describe it. It was tall and white, with long limbs and claws that were sharp as blades. It stared into me with eyes that struck the nerve of my soul. Though its mouth didn't move, it was able to speak with me somehow. I could hear its raspy voice clattering around my head like a set of die."

"That is quite the horrific picture you paint for me, Joe. What makes you think that this was different from the ordinary nightmare?" Marcus listened closely.

"It all felt so real, I could feel the cold stone under my feet, and the hairs all over my body rising towards the heavens. It was not just what I felt, it was also what the beast said that put me into a fright. The beast told me that I would be having a son, and that this son would wreak havoc across the world for many people. It told me that I would need to terminate my wife's pregnancy no matter the cost."

"I see…" Marcus bowed his head in thought. "It sounds like you were feeling the effects of one of the most emotional days of your life Joe. Why do you think you saw this creature?"

"I did speculate that this was just a vision, a nightmare, but clearly, I haven't been able to shake the thought that it was real. This is why I have come to you. My mind has been spiraling with questions about that evening. What if this beast was right and my child will end up doing these terrible things? How would I be able to go about telling my wife and my family that we would need to have an abortion because of something I very well may have dreamed up?"

"I believe that what you saw and felt must have had very real sensations to them Joe. I do not doubt the existence of beings that send us messages in our dreams. We are all a part of this living world, and if the world wants to tell us something, then it always gets its message to us. Whether or not we are able to interpret its meaning, is the question. To me, it matters not whether what you saw was indeed a dream or whether it happened in this reality. Regardless of the substance, what you saw that evening has meaning to you. What kind of meaning is what we need to discover Joe."

"I understand you Marcus," the man responded. "It may have been a reaction to the emotions of the day, or my fear of becoming a father. I've been thinking of having this child with my wife for so long that I assumed everything would unfold perfectly once we got that positive test result. Once we finally got the good news, I may have become overwhelmed with thoughts that I would not be able to lead a perfect life for my child in the ways I hoped. I felt immense pressure that I would need to do everything as a perfect role model from here on out. I doubted my ability to raise a child in this world."

"I too have felt this pressure, Joe. In the end, all we can do is put forth our best effort to do whatever nature requires us to do. Whether we have many children or none, our purpose will be served by following our own paths. Perhaps it is your requirement to have this child and to lead them on a life that will be deemed fulfilling. It is also indeed possible that you will have a child who turns into the tyrant about whom you have been foretold. I know well the pain of having a child stray the path that I have tried to steer them down. I tried for many years to teach my child about justice, and what this world requires to be right. I felt failure when my child strayed so far from my desired path that it caused him harm. The path that I envisioned for him did not become his path. In the end, the only way I could be affected was if I let myself continue to feel the pain of knowing I'd failed my child. I had to endure to do the things that this world was requiring of me."

The man responded, "I'm sorry you had to deal with such a thing Marcus. I'm struggling to imagine the pain of having a child who will not listen to reason, to what I know is right. I wonder if it would be better to have a child stray down the wrong path than it would be to not have a child at all."

"Every time Joe, I would pick having a child. The lows may have been devastating, but there was nothing like the highs that I experienced when I thought about the hopes and dreams that I had for my boy."

"Interesting," the man said with a thoughtful look on his face as if this conversation were leading to breakthroughs for him. "So, do you believe in God? Do you think this could have been some sort of prophet coming to me and warning me of the future? I've heard of things like this happening before, a premonition coming to a mortal from the sky to warn of dreadful things to come."

"Not just devastating things, but also of things most grand and good. I am not sure whether I believe in the God you or others believe in. I believe in higher power that put us here to do a job in accordance with our world. We are all here with purpose, and nothing that happens to us is due to coincidence. All that happens is a result of what must happen in order for life to continue. So, do I think some higher power or the world was telling you something when you saw the vision that night? Perhaps, but it also certainly may have simply been a creation of your own mind and stress. Interestingly, the content of what you heard was directed at assisting the greater good of this world. Your vision was worried about what may happen to the people of the future, that your son may counter their happiness somehow. It is plausible that this would be something the world would come to you with, if it were worried of an event occurring in the future."

The man answered, "You speak of the world as if it were a being in itself. I have not thought of the world in this way before. Perhaps it would be for the benefit of all if all beings worked towards the greater good of the world we live in. Surely, I would fail in my role if I were to raise a child to do such terrible things. I was not raised in any such way Marcus;

my mother and father were good to me, and they taught me well. They taught me how to treat a person the right way, caring after strangers and making sure that I was not passing off my problems onto any other person. They taught me to be thankful for the person I am, and for what I have in this life. I have never wished to harm another person. I struggle to conceive of how I could even raise a child to do these awful things of which the beast spoke of."

"As I have said, it is not always evil which breeds its own kind. If people were originally made good, evil must have developed out of that good along the way. As absolutely as there is good in this world, there will always be evil to go with it because that is the way of the world. It is not our job to get angry at this evil, it is our job to accept its existence. It would be foolish of us to expect that the world would contain nothing but good, we know of evil and have seen what it can do. Wars, famine, pointless deaths and such."

The man remarked, "Well if it is true that all things happen with reason, then it must have been meant to be for my wife to get pregnant with our child. I know not whether the visions I saw were the world talking to me, or whether it was my anxieties of becoming a father manifesting themselves into a beastly figure. I'm glad that you were willing to listen to what I have told you today, Marcus. I know that what I saw sounds insane. I truly have been feeling as if I've been going mad thinking this over for the last few days."

"Thank you for coming in and sharing this information with me Joe, I am happy to listen to whatever is causing you trouble. Believe me, I have heard far scarier tales throughout my career. You have nothing to worry about as you are in good hands. Trust the position that the world has put you in, you have been placed here for good reason. I cannot give you all of the answers to your issues, but I can at least tell you that much."

The man smiled at Marcus and slowly turned out of his chair and walked out the door behind him. He walked back down the hallway and took a long gaze at the paintings and sculptures that covered the office. They did create a very relaxing atmosphere that gave great appeal to the thinking being. The man felt better about what he was going through after his conversation with Marcus. He was convinced that he was not crazy for what he had seen, but the feeling still lingered that there may have been legitimate meaning to the visions. The man strode earnestly out into the dark rainy night.

Utopia

It was about a month into the woman's pregnancy when the family decided that they would benefit by spending a trip together in the mountains. There was a nice collection of alps just a few hours south of where they lived. In previous summers, they all made a point of carving out a week in their busy schedules so that they could go and enjoy family time together. The past two years, the family was not able to make these trips because of the issues the man and the woman were having in their attempts to conceive.

The mountain range to the south was one of flourishing life. A utopia of sorts, it was the kind of place that one would dream about when yearning for a calm day of peaceful relaxation and enjoyment. It was especially beautiful as spring began to slowly turn to summer. By this time the leaves on the trees had fully formed, and they presented a vibrant new green to all those lucky enough to take sight of them. They created a lush green canopy that rose higher as the mountain sloped up, the green of the trees almost blending into the calm blue skies that hugged the mountain peaks. The trees were so tightly packed together that from afar, the forest looked like a fuzzy rug drawn out across the landscape.

The mountain rocks took on a dark red hue and rose steeply above the trees. One could stand at the base of the rocks looking up and not be able to see where they ended. Around the base, the rocks were pearly smooth, but they became rugged as the mountain stretched into the sky above. The roasted look of the mountain contrasted nicely with the lush green and the cool blue sky. Along with the sky-blue perimeter came the melodic sounds of birds chirping. It was not a constant chirp, rather a sporadic and peaceful one that kept the listener in anticipation of the next verse. Several different kinds of birds would grace the region for the summer. It was known as one of the best bird watching spots in the nation, which would draw in crowds of people who respected the landscape and visited in hopes of catching a rare sight.

Cool flowing lakes were scattered around the mountain and the surrounding forest. The crystalline waters were so inviting that visitors were tempted to take a sip. Some went so far as to bathe in the waters to cool off after lengthy hikes on the numerous paths through the mountains. No lake stretched so wide that you could not see across to the forest on the other side. All of the lakes were teeming with life and activity. Many visitors would take canoes and small boats out onto them to enjoy the water, and some would find delight in fishing in the depths of the lakes.

The fish in the lakes were well fed and flourished. For as many different birds that flew into the area, there was an equivalent number of fish that made homes in the peaceful waters under the mountain. Fishermen were known to come to the area in search of bass that grew to incredible sizes. Like the bird watchers, the fishermen who visited would respect the environment they were approaching. They acknowledged that they were entering the home of another, and they showed great caution not to disturb the fruits of the land.

Fish were not the only creatures who enjoyed life by the water. There were bears, deer, and large cats that could be found sipping from the edges of the water or taking quick swims. These animals never seemed too disturbed by the other activity going on in the area, they were content to stay in their own routines and enjoy their surroundings. They were not hunted; it was illegal in this mountainous region to carry any weaponry. This gave the animals a peaceful mindset and their presence was appreciated by all.

There were no hotels in the area, and not many stores either. People who would come to visit would make their way to campgrounds which could hold hundreds of occupants at a time. In the warmer seasons, these grounds would quickly become flourishing hotspots for venturers from all around the globe. It was customary to bring your own tent and supplies to keep you through the duration of the stay. Some of the tents that people would bring were fascinating, almost the size of small homes. Despite the number of people that visited, there always seemed to be enough room for everyone to be able to fit comfortably.

There was a kindness between strangers in these campgrounds. Those who had never laid eyes on one another would be quick to smile and nod at their fellow travelers as they passed by each other. The more adventurous would strike up conversation and hear tales from other distant lands. If there was a group in need, whether it be setting up a tent or a few extra rations of food, there was always a neighboring crew that was quick to come to their aid. It was the kind of place that you always left in a better mood than you arrived in. On this occasion, man hoped that some quality relaxation at these campgrounds would help soothe the mental burden he had been carrying.

It was a few days after his visit with Marcus that his family came to him with the idea of the trip down to these mountains. Still pondering his conversation with the therapist, the man found himself diving deeper into the mental maze that he developed. For all of this thought he had been wrapped up in, everyone around him seemed to be cheerful. The woman continued with her happy return to the workplace and seemed to be doing better than ever. She quickly surpassed the sales numbers for the previous three months in just a matter of weeks, and she was already working on developing a new style of bedroom fit for a newborn. The man's parents were calling to check in every day and even had time to stop in for a few visits. Whenever they would come by, smiles laced their faces, and when they could not make it over, you could hear their smiles through the phone.

"It's about time we unpacked the old family tradition of heading down to the mountains! Come on, we can afford a quick trip down there this weekend. You are doing great with your career and Meredith is back to working hard as well. You both deserve a break after what you have gone through," said the man's father over the phone as he spoke with his son early one morning. There was not much that could be said to stop the man's father once he had an idea rolling. He was an assertive type, and he was very good at getting people to stick to the plans he carefully crafted. Even an impromptu plan could turn into a memorable weekend.

The woman was thrilled to get back to the mountains as well. She always loved visiting, and she saw the trip as one of the beautiful things that being part of the man's family brought into her life. As a young girl, she spent most of her vacations with her sisters in the small apartment building that they shared with their mother. She would always be disappointed when her classmates would joyously proclaim that they were leaving the city for the beach or some other exotic location. She knew that her family did not have the money to take such trips. She was grateful, however, that she was able to spend her breaks alongside her mother and her sisters. Now, the woman still smiled when she remembered the first time that the man's family brought her to the beautiful mountains.

The woman was finishing up packing as she prepared for departure when out of nowhere, she heard a ring floating through the air. Her heart leapt; she had been thinking recently of her sisters. While before she had trepidation and uncertainty as to what their conversation would entail, she had recently become eager to talk with them. She sprinted to the phone and picked it up with a wide grin, "Hello! Meredith speaking."

"Meredith, it's your sister Martha, long time no talk. Where have you been and how are you doing? I've missed hearing your voice. Mother, Elizabeth, and I have been wondering when we would be hearing from you," the woman's sister said with a voice of relief.

"Martha, I have missed you all dearly. I'm sorry that I didn't call earlier. I had been going through a lot as Joe and I were struggling to conceive for some time. But I'm pregnant now, I feel happy again and I felt bad that I hadn't called to let you all know how I was doing," Meredith responded, even more relieved.

Time seemed to fly from there as the two women got right back to talking as if they were having a conversation on their regular walk back from school to their tiny apartment. Around the house you could hear the joy flowing from the woman as she caught up with her beloved sister and told her about the trip to the mountains that she was excited to embark on. In no time, the man was tapping the woman on the shoulder and letting her know that it was time to leave.

They were taking the man's father's jeep down to the mountains. This was another one of the relics of the past, taking down the doors to the jeep and enjoying the open air as they zoomed down the highway. Of course, storage was not great with this vehicle, so they had to attach a turtle shell on top and hope that it did not go flying in the dust behind them. Besides, they did not pack much, as they were looking forward to spending a lot of quality time with each other in conversation and thought. The road seemed empty for most of the ride down. The trees brimmed with a cool green on the side of the road, blurry as the group trekked speedily by. They were eager to get to the camp and begin a much-needed vacation.

As they got closer to the base of the mountain and the site of the campground, they began to see the wonderous mountain landscape. They caught glimpses of people patrolling the woods and looking for new adventures amongst the tall trees. Flashes of small animals including squirrels and birds got the family excited and the familiar chirping from the birds began to fill the air. The forest was as lush as ever, and they could hardly see through the dense green shield that it created. With focus, however, the crystal blue of the lake in the background appeared to them.

As the group caught sight of the campground, they could not help the grins from encompassing their faces. "We're here!" the man's father yelled out victoriously. He had made the drive down in record time. They quickly spotted a lovely place in the campground as if the spot had been reserved for them. Immediately, the crew got out and began to unpack the few materials they brought. They each thought of the old days when none of them knew how to pitch a tent, and laughed at the ease with which they were able to put them up now. It was not too crowded in the campground, but there were just enough people to make it feel like a safe camping experience. Smiles were exchanged and the family quickly began to decide what they would do first.

"I want to head down to the lake to see the beautiful sparkling blue water, oh how I have missed it," the man's mother was the first to speak. As often is the case, first to speak creates the law of the land. So, with that the group gathered up a few small things: snacks, novels, and some sunscreen, and they went towards a carved-out path that they knew led to the water's edge. They were mostly silent on the short walk to the lake, being sure to take in the sounds of nature that washed over them. Deep breathing filled their lungs with fresh air and cleared their minds of miniscule worries. They were together, and that was all they needed to be happy in that moment.

As they approached the edge of the water, they were lucky enough to see a family of deer off in the distance taking sips from the lake. Extra carefully and quietly, they approached them so as not to startle them away. Both parties respected each other's location, and although there was a mere 20 feet between them, they both continued business as usual. It was a serenity that they had missed while they were going about their fast-paced lives closer to the city.

The family gazed out towards the lake, which was stunning on a sunny day like today. The surface of the lake gleamed with sunlight and rippled lightly with the activity that was taking place upon it. There were a few small boats out with families basking in the sun and slowly paddling around the lake. It was a large lake, requiring a panoramic scan to take it all in. Especially spectacular was the mountain that reflected across a large portion of the lake. It was looking especially red that day, with clay that would sift under the hands like powder. It stood tall into the sky and past the clouds which were puffy and white. There were even a few brave souls climbing the mountain to try and get an even better view of the surrounding utopia.

The family stood at the water's edge and took it all in, breathing deeply and exhaling calmly. The slow ripple of the lake made for an excellent backdrop as they collectively soothed their minds from the storm which provoked them for so long. After looking out into the pearly blue waters for a moment longer, the man's father unexpectedly took off towards the water and dove headfirst. He broke the water's plane like an eagle dropping below the surface in search of food. In a flash, he disappeared beneath the watery veil of the lake.

The rest of the family stood watching as his head resurfaced with a huge smile. They all began to laugh, never ceasing to be amazed at what the old man could come up with out of thin air. With that, one by one they all decided they would jump into the lake and join him. Fully clothed and with reckless abandonment, they leapt for joy into a flurry of crashing waves. They splashed around in the water with glee, it was just deep enough for them to touch the bottom with their toes. For what seemed like eternities, they swam together and enjoyed the day.

Once they finally got out of the water and dried off, the rest of the day seemed to fly by like fishing line coming of a reel with a great swordfish on the hook. They made their way back to the camp by the time the sun began to set around the beautiful mountain. This was around the hour that most of the campground's visitors would return to their stations for an evening of fun and games. Hundreds of people all eating dinner with their families at the same time made for quite the lively experience. There were songs to be sung, hugs to be shared, and memories to be recalled.

The family had big plans for dinner as they gathered up wood to throw into the fire pit that was conveniently placed in the center of the station they had claimed. Every station had a fire pit, and there was endless firewood around the grounds so that each group could enjoy warm, comforting flames as they settled into the dark night. The man and his mother went to gather wood for the fire while the man's father and the woman stayed to help prepare a large lake trout which they were graciously gifted by one of the neighboring groups. "We got too many out there today, here's one for you."

Within no time, there was a roaring fire set up, crackling with sparks into the deep purple of the night sky. The orange laughter of the flames soared higher as the freshly filleted trout was rested upon them. Stomachs growled with anticipation as the skin of the fish began to crispen. A few minutes later, everyone had a plate with more than they could eat. About a pound of trout on each dish, with half a can of black beans and corn to wash it down. It was as good as it gets.

This was the time around the campgrounds where everything started to get quieter, besides the clatter of utensils against plates of food. The visitors filled their stomachs to their hearts' content, and if anyone needed more there was a plethora of rations. It seemed as if the food there never ran out. The family took glances at each other and smiled as they continued to scarf down the delicious feast that they created with their own hands. There was a feeling of success in making their own meal, not having to depend on anyone else to sustain themselves.

At last came the time when everyone finished their meals and began to settle back into the dark night. The sounds of crickets chirping became more evident. Looking closely into the sky would reveal the occasional bat darting through the open air. There were no large trees covering the grounds, just an open window to the night sky which spanned the entire area. A bed of stars blanketed the sky, twinkling bright and uninhibited by city lights. One could look into this sky for hours without becoming bored or dissatisfied. In fact, some people would bring their telescopes, which were used to spot other planets which spun millions of miles away from the rock they inhabited.

Finally, the family took their eyes away from the beauty of the surrounding nature, and returned to the conversation they had been enjoying throughout the day. Conversation was different, however, at this hour of the evening. The thoughts had shifted from the joyous events of the day to remembering the past and what they were looking forward to in the future.

"I can't say enough how happy I am that you two are finally through with that dark chapter of your lives," the man's father chimed in. "I have been waiting to have a grandchild for what feels like an eternity. Your mother and I were so concerned about you two, and now we can see that life has returned to your eyes."

"Yes, ever since your brother, we have been especially worried that we wouldn't be able to live to see you carrying on the lessons that we taught you," the man's mother offered as a tear slipped down her cheek and spilled onto the grassy carpet beneath her. This comment caused the rest of the family to gaze into the fire with glossy eyes. "Your father always talks about leaving his legacy on this earth, and how he wants his lessons to pass on so that he will be remembered."

"Yes, I find that my time here may have been wasted if you two weren't able to continue the storyline that your mother and I instilled in you," the man's father cut in. "I have done my father proud by raising you to become a good man. That is how my father and his fathers will be remembered. It's important to me that I leave my positive mark on this world. I hope that others remember me for the hard work and kindness that I have shown them. I have a feeling that you can be great, my son, and your child can follow you. With the success that you have shown in your architectural career, our family name could be hailed for many generations to come."

The man responded, "I do not deny that I've had remarkable success in the field so far, but I am not interested in having my name known by strangers thousands of years from now. What good does it do the family if we are remembered anyway? We will all end up dying like the millions of people that came before us. Our job is simply to continue producing for the good of humanity, and to enjoy and love our families while we are here. Of course, it would be great to have a child and pass along those virtues to them so that they can enjoy their lives, but the pursuit should not be for fame and future namesake."

"Is that all we are here to do, to work and to enjoy our time? We need to strive to be great people, to have our names go down in history as those that will be remembered forever. We do need to work hard for the people of this world, and for that we will be appreciated and remembered. If our bloodline runs out, there are no more of our virtues being passed along in this world. What good are our contributions if they all end up forgotten as relics of the past?" the man's father spoke back.

"Our names may be forgotten, but the lessons that we teach our offspring will continue. It is not important whether we receive credit for our successes from those who have not yet been born. Countless lives have been forgotten, but we are still living in the ways that they taught themselves and others to live. The evidence that teachings of the past live on is seen in many aspects of our society. Look around you, there is order, there is care for the other strangers who have visited these grounds. They do so not so that they may be remembered for the kindness in their actions, but because they are helping humanity advance by nourishing those whom they do not know," the man responded.

"I am afraid of being forgotten on this earth my son. What is my life worth if it will not be remembered. I want our name to be labeled across buildings for centuries to come, so that people will know what we have given to humanity. That is why I felt such immense joy when I learned of your child on the way. We will grow old, we will die, but we need to keep our stories and our contributions alive," the man's father shook.

"Our buildings will fall, just as all structures have. Our names will not be praised, but instead just a flash in the busy lives of the people of the future. And it is not their job to obsess over recognizing those who came before them, instead, they are meant to be furthering humanity and creating their own contributions. The buildings standing nameless would be enough to inspire these people to continue to climb higher into the clouded skies. I wish to live my life as a good man, loving my family and cherishing the fleeting moments we share. The future of humanity is important to me, but I do not need them to know my name," the man explained.

"They will know our name because we will strive to be great my son. It is the great man that goes down in history. It is the great men of the past who have changed the way that we look at the world. How could we aspire only to be good when we have the gifts and the dedication to be great?"

"And at what cost is that greatness achieved? These great men you speak of have surely sacrificed time with their families in the present so that they could go down in history. The cost of future generations being familiar with your name will be the memories which you could have been making in the present. The love that could have been shared. All so that there will be an extra name in the history books or alongside the road. Many lose themselves pursuing greatness when all they truly desire is to live the life of a good person," the man said.

"I feel the drive within me to be great, my son, and I can see in your eyes that you feel it as well. I see it in the way that you have worked your craft, you are miles ahead of those who graduated with you. There are men who have been working at this craft for a lifetime and could not dream of ascending to the heights that you have already surpassed. You will be great, and so will my grandchild. I will have it no other way," responded the man's father.

"The way you two bicker over something that does not matter. A good man who loves his family and spends his days getting to know them or a great man who works tirelessly at his craft in hopes of being remembered, tonight will not decide which one either of you turn out to be," the man's mother chuckled. "This back and forth reminds me of the times your brother used to chime in and break up the feud with some lighthearted banter. We should be appreciative of the things that have already happened in our lives, the gifts that we have been blessed with. Let us remember the past this evening, let us remember our beloved son." With that comment the mood softened, and the group looked back towards the flame as the corners of their mouths began to lift.

****

It was the hottest part of the summer as the family drove up to the beach to make their yearly trip. There was always a bit of traffic on the way out, but they did not mind, they were so focused on the week that awaited them. The large rental homes that could fit the entire family, the outdoor showers that meant a day at the beach had come to an end, and the sounds of seagulls floating about the clear blue skies above. These were the thoughts that pleasantly drifted through their heads as they gazed into the bumpers of other vehicles on the highway.

By the time they arrived, their hearts were beating so hard that they almost burst out of their chests. The excitement had grown to the point of needing to jump out of the car and run their feet through the soft sand surrounding the rental home. Quickly, the children would run into the home to claim their bedroom for the week, hoping that they would all be able to fit into one of the rooms. They anticipated the late nights of conversation, laughs, playing games, and drinking their favorite beverage, the Shirley Temple. After claiming their room, the kids would quickly move onto the entertainment selection. Would it be a collection of movies, a television series, or video games? Whatever it was, there were always smiles draped across the faces of all of them as they played late into the evenings.

The first night always ended in pizza. The family was so large that they had to get at least five boxes to fill everyone. Everyone munched gleefully until they felt full. There were always leftovers to be had in case a late-night hunger struck. Those late hours were when a lot of the best fun occurred. On a few occasions, the family had such a good time laughing with each other that the neighbors threatened to call the police. These threats were baseless, however, and there was not a night that did not hear the laughter of the children.

The days that would follow were occupied by afternoons spent laid out on the beach under the shining sun. Often there was not a cloud in the sky as the family staked out a spot among a fleet of umbrellas. When hunger struck, they would always have a cooler full of freshly made sandwiches to fuel them with more energy to get back into the bustling waves of the serene blue ocean. There were days when the waves violently thrashed back and forth along the shoreline, some of which brought the greatest laughs. The children stood patiently waiting for a giant wave to surface from the ocean, one that would sweep them from their feet as they laughed back towards the shore. The eldest brother was always the best at standing his ground as the giant waves crashed around him. Many times, the rest of the children would be swept away by the ferocious liquid storm, only to look back and see him still standing tall like a tower amidst a light breeze.

Nights on the beach would end in wiffle ball tournaments played between the whole family. Everyone got their chance to get involved in the game, which always seemed to come down to the final moments to decide the victor. No matter who came out victoriously, it was all about the fun that was had throughout the game. Waves would crash in the background as the sun set opposite the fine ocean line that swept across the perimeter of the earth. The eldest brother was not the most skilled out on the playing field, but he was always a player to be selected early in the family draft. His determination was unparalleled, and he always seemed to find himself involved in some of the games' most pivotal moments. It was a joy to watch him giving his best efforts.

Of course, most nights would end with the crew taking the walk down to their favorite amusement park which always seemed to be well situated about 15 minutes from the rentals. The park was well lit throughout the night, with guests running around with fistfuls of tickets and dripping ice cream cones. There was so much joy going around at that little amusement park. It did have a few rides to choose from, but for the family, the main attraction was the arcade.

The walls of the arcade were lined with many claw machines that were filled with plush characters from the most popular current media. Only the arcade would be able to tell how many dollars were spent trying to acquire the treasure resting just beyond the glass of the machine. Some nights, the family would make it a competition to see who could collect the most prizes. Surely, those were the nights where most of the money was spent on these beloved trips. On later occasions, the goal would be to collect tickets and save up the whole week to spend them all on one big prize. The best they could do was a large dragon figure whose whereabouts remain unknown to this day. It was all good fun, and the end of the night had the troop strolling back victoriously to their home.

That was what these rentals felt like to the children, home. The houses may have been occupied by different families each week, but for the week that the family was in town, there was no place on the island that felt more comfortable for them. It was a true power of the eldest brother to make those around him feel as if they were at home, even in the most foreign of environments.

****

One memory shined vividly in the minds of the family sitting around the fire at the campsite on that fateful night. They remembered a time in which they were all gathered in the backyard, celebrating as they often did. One of the events for the day was a competition: filling up a mug of water and holding it out with a straight arm for as long as possible. It may sound like an easy feat, but after a few minutes one realizes that it takes herculean willpower to keep an arm aloft. Long after the rest of the family members put down their arms, the eldest brother stood tall and strong with his arm fully extended towards them. The competition was won, but he still had that look of determination on his face. He wanted to hold his arm out for as long as he could. He wanted to show his family how strong he really was. And so, he did.

As the family gazed into the crackling fire, tears filled their eyes, soft smiles filled their faces, and love filled their hearts.

9
Searching

It had been a few weeks since the family returned from their trip to the mountain. They all felt refreshed upon their return. They were grateful to be able to spend time together. For the most part, they all had busy lives at home and so they were not often able to enjoy each other's company for long periods of time.

Things were going smoothly for the man and woman as they continued living blissfully, knowing that their child would be arriving in due time. The woman was able to spend time with her sisters and mother through video calls. They were all happy to hear from the woman, they had missed her dearly. Plans were made for the group to reunite in celebration of the woman having her child. Her sisters had also been lucky enough to become mothers in the recent years, something about which the woman was initially resentful. She could not understand why she had not been given the same gift that her sisters took for granted. Now, with the woman bringing a child of her own into the mix, the sisters grew joyful thinking of the times that their children would share together in the future.

The man had been trying to focus on the rigors of finding new architectural work, but with time passing he could not evade the feeling that it would eventually become too late before he could act. The thoughts of his visions began to slowly creep back into his mind after getting back from the respite of vacation with his family. As he returned to reality, he once again remembered the ideas that began to drive him mad. If he were to act and ask for his wife to terminate her pregnancy, it would have to be soon. At this point, it was a little over a month since the woman was declared pregnant, so the man knew that if he waited a month or two longer his time for a decision would have passed.

The man sat in his office chair and looked to his hands that hovered over the leather arms of his chair. He was once again happy that he was able to enjoy the comforts of home throughout the day. Outside the window, rain steadily fell. It had not ceased for some time. There was no letup in the steady fall, battering the pavement as more puddles began to sprout. Drops covered the window enough to make it difficult for the man to see outside into his beloved yard. For this he was resentful.

As the man continued to look around his vast brown office, he decided that it was time to do a bit more research on what he saw. He sat there, not completely satisfied with the information received from Marcus. It was difficult whether to tell if the man was receiving a message from the universe, or whether he was succumbing to the pressures of becoming a father. The man figured that he would search for others that saw similar visions or felt comparable things upon hearing that they would become first time fathers or mothers.

Upon initial search, the man was able to find recounts of many who claimed they were extremely overwhelmed when hearing that they would be having a child. There were some who screamed with joy, some who fainted, and even those who decided to run away from their families after getting the news. For many, the revelation that they would become a parent seemed to be one of great joy. On the other hand, there were those who did not wish to become a parent or those who did not feel ready to complete such an arduous task. Even for those who felt great joy at the notion of becoming a parent, there were plenty of people reporting a great deal of nervousness and anxiety.

The man was able to find some stories told by people who had dreams about the future of their parenthood. Many claim that they dreamed of their children and were able to accurately describe what their child would look like before the child was even born. Others dreamt of having their partner or children taken away from them and figured that they dreamt this way because they did not feel worthy or prepared enough to be a partner or parent at the time. The man searched for hours, but he could not find any stories quite like that of the one he experienced. Nothing reported about any beasts coming to future parents in the night and proclaiming that their future young one would kill off millions.

The sight of the beast flickered before the man's eyes; he could automatically recall the look of its slim white figure shining in the night. He tried searching the internet for any kind of beast that looked identical, but to no avail. He wondered how it could be that he dreamed this beast out of his mind's oblivion, having never seen anything that looked quite like it. There was information online stating that the mind could not dream of something that the person had never seen in their past, but the man could not recall seeing this white figure at any point in his life.

Eventually, the man's search brought him to a tale well-known throughout human history. This was that of the angel that appeared to Joseph before he was to become the father of Jesus, the son of God. Had the man been more of a religious follower, he may have thought of the relation between his dream and the story of Joseph and the angel sooner. When he saw these search results, his mind flooded with the old Bible stories that he was told by his parents growing up.

He remembered how Joseph dreamt of an angel appearing to him and telling him to wed Mary, the mother of Jesus. The angel told Joseph of how Mary would be having a child without first having sex. Further, the angel told Joseph that this child, Jesus, would be the savior of the world. Joseph was obedient to the angel, doing as he was told. The rest remains history, and what the angel said in Joseph's dream ended up coming true.

The man thought of the similarities between the story of Joseph, and what he had gone through on that fateful night. He too, believed that he was dreaming when the monster came to him in the night. Perhaps it was not a monster, but instead an angel of the same kind that visited Joseph so long ago. There are tales in the Bible of the angels having the faces of many beasts when they appear to the humans. The man's beast did not have multiple faces, but surely the one that it did have was nothing like a face that the man had seen before. He remembered the white blank stare that he received in his backyard as the cool wind danced around his motionless body. Shivers started to run down his spine as he thought of the icy cold drops of sweat that slid down his arms which he could not move.

Just as the angel had come to Joseph with a promise about the future of the son, Jesus, the beast came to the man and told him what his future child would bring to the world. Jesus would be a savior, as the angel foretold. What would become of the man's child whom the beast predicted to bring evil to the world? The man remembered how the beast instructed him to terminate the pregnancy of his wife at any costs. He thought of what the repercussions would be for him if he followed obediently, as worked out for Joseph.

Or perhaps this was no angel at all that came to the man in the dead of night, but instead a demon of sorts. The man began to research what kinds of demons may be the parallel to the angel that came to Joseph. He read of those who used trickery and deceit to get what they desired, at the expense of the humans whom the demons worked to fool. These demons fed off the fear of the humans, and they would relentlessly assault their minds with visions of false truths and promises. The man thought of his fears of becoming a father. It was just as plausible that a demon may have come to him in the night to attempt to feast upon his fear.

If an angel were able to visit a human, then it seemed not too far a stretch that a demon would be able to make that same journey across the dark night sky. The man wondered if he had been lied to by one of these demons that evening. Surely the look and the feel of this creature was one that evinced a sense of horror. He remembered the feeling of nothingness that he experienced when he tried to look into the monster. A feeling that there was no redemption in those dark eyes, and nothing that could save him in that frightening moment.

And if it had been a demon that came to the man that night, why had an angel not come to show him the correct path. Would an angel not choose to appear and counter the evil seed that was planted in the mind of the man? The man wondered why he was left to his own devices when having to make the decision on whether what he saw was real or not. It would be pure evil to trick the man into ending his wife's pregnancy without a viable reason.

It was at this point that the man decided he needed to take a step away from his research to collect what he had found. At this stage there were no definitive answers. He continued to feel lonesome in attempts to figure out what occurred. He was used to being dropped into a situation without any specific road map for where he should be headed. That was why he created such a name for himself in the architectural field. Often, he would receive jobs that did not involve blueprints, but instead just an idea conveyed from the client to the man. The man was extremely skilled in bringing to life even the most outlandish ideas for buildings that clients would request he build.

He thought back to a time when he was approached by a group of devout pastors who wished to create a gargantuan temple that resembled the shape of a dove. The man searched days for another builder who had previously been successful in completing such an arduous task. As hard as he looked, he found that this type of building was uncharted territory in the profession. Upon hearing this, the pastors were persistent in their demand that a building be shaped in a way that would give hope to the guests that occupied it. They would not budge on the idea, telling the man that they would look for services elsewhere if he could not provide what they were looking for.

The man took this as a challenge. He quickly configured ways to create multiple shapes and put them together to give a bird-like appearance to the building. It was an extremely difficult task which ended up spanning over two years longer than originally expected. By the end of the process, the pastors were delighted with the building that the man built for them. His hard work paid off, and more unique building shape ideas started to come in from all over the land. Word spread, and that is how the man ended up with the title of "The Unique Creator".

Now the man thought of that title, and he thought of what he said to his father back at the campground while on vacation. If he was able to make such unique creations, then he believed he should be able to figure out what to do with the issue that presented itself in regard to his wife's pregnancy. Try as he may, he was not able to find anyone on the internet who had the same experience that he had on that fateful evening. He was a pioneer in alien waters, with the job of steadying his ship amongst waves of delusion.

He also thought about how this title, "The Unique Creator", would play out in the future. For all his knowledge, there may have been another such creator in the past who was now long forgotten. Perhaps the nickname was really one of secondhand quality. Surely, the creators of the ancient pyramids may have held equal claim to the title. Was he really worthy of such a title that had been given to him by those who had not experienced all of creation?

He then turned his mind to the selfish selection that he had been preparing to make since the night of the visit. If this prophecy did come true, would he be without fault regarding the slaughter that would come to millions at the hand of his child? He could not claim that he had no idea what would occur. The man could not play the victim after hearing the future spoken so vividly. Yet, he was swayed towards the selfish option of keeping his rekindled family joy alive. He did not want to lose out on times such as the evening his family experienced the night that they found out about the pregnancy. He did not want to feel his family's pain when he told them that he would be trying to convince his wife to terminate her pregnancy. He did not want to go back to a place where the woman and he loathed each other's existence. All of this would make the man's life far more difficult. Still, however, what if the reward for doing such a thing would be saving the lives of countless people in the future?

The man had spoken about how he would try to impact the future without needing the recognition for it. He talked at the campground about how it mattered not what the people of the future thought or remembered from those of the past as individuals. Rather, the lessons and virtues that were passed down to future generations were of greater importance. He thought, what better way to impact the future than to save the lives of so many. No one would ever know of the sacrifice that he made for it to be that way. The joys of being able to raise a child in a loving family. More vacations with a new comrade, smiles and laughs to be shared around more campgrounds for years to come. Would he be willing to give this future up in order to ensure a brighter future for the lives of many?

The man thought back to the wonderful childhood he was fortunate to have while living with his parents. Whatever he needed as a young boy, his parents would always be quick to get for him. Whether it was an ice cream treat on a broiling summer day at the pool, or an opportunity to take the reins on a new job in the workshop, the answer was always yes. They wanted to see him happy. As a future parent, he was already softening to the idea of wanting to see his child happy. He felt himself falling in love with the child who was not yet born. The man did not want to betray his child and end their life prematurely. If this was the bond that he felt to his child only a few weeks after conception, that bond would surely grow to infinite lengths in the years to come.

He wondered if this was the same challenge that others had faced before him. Would they have chosen their own happiness rather than ensuring the safety of others? Would it be so wrong for a person to choose their own personal gain over that of strangers in a distant world?

As the man continued to ponder, sheets of rain continued to pour onto the clean glass windows around the office. The storm had picked up considerably, and it was difficult to see very far into the growing grayness. Figures appeared to create themselves and dissolve in the rain drops that raced down the outside of the house. The tall green trees in the distance were constantly battered, dancing with the wind and the rain. Puddles continued to form as the grass beneath them pressed into the earth slowly drowning.

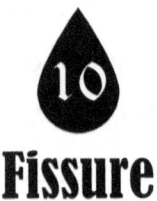

Fissure

A new day brought the same gray atmosphere as the man and woman awoke in their room to the steady drizzle of rain outside. It was the time in the pregnancy when the two were checking for signs of the child inside the woman's stomach. There was no visible bulge yet, but the two agreed that they knew it would be coming soon. For the pair, this was very exciting as they continued their journey together and prepared to welcome their first child into the world. For the man, the constant pattering in his mind told him that he was running short on time to make his decision. It would not be long until it would no longer be viable to terminate the pregnancy. If he could wish for anything, it would be to wish for more time to make the decision on what to do. He knew, however, that time was a resource that always eluded those who tried to capture it.

It was a dreary Saturday morning as the two began to rise out of bed a bit later than their weekly schedules allowed for. There was no better feeling for them than realizing that they had a day where no tasks were due for completion. Work was off for the woman, and while the man sometimes found work on the weekends, he felt that he did not have to get anything done, at least on this rainy day. Although, he had recently been taking a lot of time off work as he continued trying to figure out his predicament. Calls and emails had come in during the week, but the man believed nothing too serious would occur if he took some time off from checking them.

In fact, there had been a job that caught his eye while he was working earlier in the week. One of his colleagues came to him with a suggestion for a new school campus to go up in the very area where the man talked with Bernard. David, the man's assistant, had discovered a start-up company which aspired to create private schools that would be placed outside the city along with a learning center where kids without homes would be able to come live and interact with the children enrolled at the private schools. David knew that the man had been looking for ways to positively impact the surrounding community, and that he was looking for something to build in the area on the outskirts of the city. It seemed like the perfect idea to the man, and he gratefully accepted an invitation to meet with the startup company to discuss it.

It was on a gray afternoon a few days later that the man received an email from the director of the company stating that they were disappointed that the man did not show up to the scheduled meeting to discuss the school project. The man was flustered, his mind had been completely occupied wondering what he should do about the predicament he was in with his future child. This was one of several deadlines that he was beginning to let slide into the forgotten regions of his mind. He apologized to the company, but they were adamant that they would be moving onward with their idea in hopes of finding a new location.

Afterwards the man was distraught. He had found an idea for buildings that he could create to influence the community in a positive way. Had he been more vigilant in pursuing the opportunity, things may have gone differently. Now, he had the job of searching once more for a project that would bring positive energy to the rural grassy area. One thing was certain, he did not want to lose the opportunity to build there and in doing so allow Bernard to go forward with his plan for the region. The man believed that the vice-ridden enterprises that Bernard proposed would not be beneficial to the lives of those in the area.

For now, however, the only thing that the man and woman had planned for the day was breakfast together. Often in the past, they would wake up on these late weekend mornings and conjure meals that were large enough to feed an army. They would eat heartily and still have enough to save for the next day. It was an enjoyable process to cook together, to create something from scratch that they could both be proud of and enjoy. The plan for this morning was to make strawberry and blueberry pancakes. This was a favorite of the woman's. She remembered times in the past when she and her sisters would make them for their mom on special occasions. The girls would laugh as they bounced around their tiny kitchen, making a mess that they knew would take hours to clean.

The man slowly turned up out of bed and looked to the woman who was still laying down. They smiled at each other, knowing that it was finally time to get the day started. They slowly made their way down to the kitchen and started up the coffee machine, needing to grease their gears before kicking into turbo for the morning cooking. The thick brown coffee that morning tasted extra delicious and perked them up a bit more, knowing that they would not be burdened with anything stressful for the rest of the day.

They sat slowly sipping as they listened to the droplets of rain bounce against the back porch. The dreariness of the day did not impact their outlook. They were determined not to let anything distract them from their breakfast plans. Often on mornings like these the two would sit reading the newspaper. They were one of the few on their street that still had a physical copy delivered. Most of the neighbors had either taken to social media for their information, or they were content not to see what was happening in the world around them. This morning though, the two sat on their phones scrolling through the day's news. They did not want to venture into the rain to retrieve the paper and put an early damper on the day.

The couple was never too concerned about the news and what was happening in the world surrounding the town in which they lived in. For them, outside news was only a distraction that did not need to be present throughout the day. The main reason that they read the news was to have something to converse about between themselves and with their peers at work. It was always nice to have something to talk about. Rather than the world outside the town, the pair was instead focused on what they could do to impact the lives of the people and the place in which they lived.

There was nothing too out of the ordinary in this week's edition of the news. The forecast was calling for more rain throughout the next week, with the usual advice of "trying to stay dry". The weather section noted that the area would continue to see record rainfall, a dreary rain that had not let up for what seemed like months. There were a few stories about crime rates rising in the city. It was generally a calm city in which neighbors could trust each other, but it seemed that things were taking a turn for the worse. Other stories ranged from the development of electric cars to the potential space exploration to come. To the man, these stories were interesting reads, but he did not truly understand the gravity of them. He was a builder, he understood how to build.

He was about to get to his regular viewing of the housing section when the woman got up and announced she was ready to get the pancakes going. With that, they both flung down their phones and got to work. They carefully secured their matching aprons as they turned the lights and appliances on in the kitchen. The woman grabbed the pancake mix from its usual spot in the cabinet, and the man dug into the fridge and unveiled the blueberries and strawberries. They always did their best to keep fresh fruit around, which they purchased from the local farmers market around the corner. They swore that this was the best fruit they ever tasted, a notion to which many of their guests agreed.

The succulent fruit was chopped up. The milk, eggs, and pancake mix were thrown together in a bowl. The two took turns whisking it all together while simultaneously working through the side dishes for the morning. Fresh bacon sizzled on the stovetop and a browning tray of home fries sat in the oven. The aroma of a great breakfast started to fill the air as the pair remembered to breathe deeply and enjoy the moment they were having together. A large pancake pan was buttered up and put on the range. While they waited for the pan to heat up, the table was set with sweet maple syrup and a warmed stick of salted butter. Chopped citrusy oranges and washed red grapes were placed in the center of the table.

When the time came for the pancakes to hit the pan, the woman carefully scooped out a perfect portion of the pancake mix and placed it into a circle on the hot plate. The sizzle and smell that came from the cooking cake was heavenly. A mixture of sweet dough combined with fresh fruit, one could not find a better smelling breakfast in all the land. The cakes sat on the stove for a bit longer until they were flipped by the woman. This was a recipe she perfected, and she always knew when to flip the cakes over. The result was, without fail, a golden crispy pancake with chunks of strawberries and blueberries dug into the gooey yet flaky interior. A few minutes later both sides of the treat sported the same lovely golden hue.

Quickly after the pancakes were removed from the heat and put onto a large porcelain serving dish, the rest of the food joined them on the dining table. Different dishes held the bacon and the home fries which were still crackling from the heat. The man and woman stood and licked their lips as they prepared for what would surely be a feast to remember. They hurried over to the cabinets in the kitchen to collect their plates and utensils and rushed back to the table where they sat on opposite ends. It was not too long of a table, short enough for them to comfortably reach into the center and scoop up their anticipated meals.

They filled their plates with stacks of pancakes, topped with gooey maple syrup and soft butter. The golden brown of the pancakes started to glisten as the butter was spread evenly over the surface of each. The syrup became hot and began to seep down into the lower levels of their pancake towers. They each added fresh grapes and oranges which accompanied the crispy bacon and home fries. The man and woman looked at each other and smiled as they began to dine from within their dimly lit kitchen.

As always, the meal was as delicious as the effort that the two chefs put into creating the feast. Once again, the two were not disappointed with their meal. They always talked of how they enjoyed their own home-cooked meals more than going out and dining. Something about the satisfaction of crafting their own food always seemed to add a touch of superiority to their dishes when compared to dishes which were brought out by a server.

When the pair finished eating, they cleaned up the kitchen as efficiently as they had dirtied it. They were a highly competent team, with the man rinsing the dishes and cookware in concert with the woman clearing the table and putting the dishes into the dishwasher. They were so in tune during the process that they began to whistle together in harmony as they excitedly anticipated the rest of their day off.

When the kitchen was fully cleaned, the woman told the man she was going out for a quick run around the block. She always enjoyed running, but she was not eager to do so during her days growing up because she was unexcited about running through busy city streets. Since the two moved into their suburban home, she had taken to running much more frequently. The man was impressed that even with a baby growing inside of her, the woman was still able to stay fit and active. Sometimes they would even join together for their runs, but today the man told her he did not have it in him.

When the man settled back into his chair at the kitchen, he looked out into the rain which had come to a lighter drizzle than the downpour they had been experiencing the last few weeks. He thought he could hear birds chirping from the backyard, but he could not see any in the birdhouse which sat lofted amongst the green trees. The sky seemed a bit brighter as if it were an off white with only a few drops of gray imbedded deep into the color formula. Slowly, the man began to smile as he felt a bit of ease for what felt like the first time since the family visited the mountains. Promptly, he remembered that he had not finished his morning read. As he picked up his phone and opened his favorite section, his mouth dropped in horror.

Right across the top of the housing section in large bold letters read, "New Plot Approved for Futuristic Retreat Sadie & Gunther's". In a flash, the man remembered his conversation with Bernard in the field on the outskirts of town. He saw the crooked smile of Bernard gazing back at him from the black letters of the headline of the article. He remembered the twisted ideas that Bernard put into his mind when he was telling the man about the plans he had for the area. A place of sinning, night life, and strip clubs condensed all so close to the spot that so many families called home. What would become of this peaceful area now that this deviant development was going to be built tall for all to see?

His first thought was one of a despicable nature towards himself. He thought of the opportunity that he had to meet with the school creators and all the good that an idea like that would have brought to the area. It would have been a place flourishing with young and thoughtful life, influencing positive growth for generations to come. How could he have let such an opportunity slip through his fingers, knowing that if he did so then Bernard's ideas may come to fruition? In fact, he had been so occupied thinking about the beast he saw on that fateful night that he completely forgot about meeting Bernard. His distracted mind obscured the goals and aspirations that he had been working on in the office. His running mind seemed to jettison the traits that brought him to the lofty stature he held within the architectural industry. Before he was relentless in pursuing new ideas, but now he was a shell of his creative self.

The man looked away from the grim newspaper into his backyard, yearning for the feeling he experienced just minutes prior. The sky was promptly darkening gray, and the rain began picking up steam like a locomotive. The drops accelerated against the glass doors and the pitter-pattering sounds began to tick through the ear canal and into the man's brain. Again, he had that feeling as if he were dreaming. The morning with his wife had gone so perfectly undisturbed, only to be thrown off a cliff at the mere sight of a sentence displayed in black ink. The man fought to remain composed, blinking his eyes repeatedly to try and wake up from yet another nightmare.

His next thought was wondering how Bernard could have gotten this project pushed through and who he convinced to help him build the place. He remembered that Bernard was a charismatic man. When the man met Bernard in the field, he was at first eager to help Bernard in his plan to build before the details of the voyage were announced. Bernard seemed like someone who could talk himself into big things, making it appear as if he had the answers to questions which he knew nothing about. Nonetheless, the man was enticed with Bernard's presentation, and he was not surprised that Bernard was quickly able to convince someone to create his monstrosity.

What was a real hurdle for the man to understand was how Bernard was able to get the job approved on this plot of land so quickly. It had not been long since the day he met Bernard, and even for a character of the man's occupational stature, getting approved to build on a lot was generally a drawn-out process. The man began to understand the answer to all his questions when he continued to dig into the article in front of him. He struggled to read the first few paragraphs of the piece, still not quite believing it to be real. It highlighted the great entrepreneur Bernard Brooks who was famous around the nation for placing new and innovative city expansions that were drawing crowds in the thousands.

According to the article, Bernard was the mind behind 25 of these sites throughout the world, and he was expanding his business model rapidly. The article noted how happiness levels in all the cities Bernard implemented his designs in were increasing dramatically. The man thought about this, and he did not see a way in which the projects that Bernard proposed would only bring positives. Sure, there would be a large group of people who enjoy the festivities, but the establishments that these structures housed could also leave a lasting negative impact on the calmer folk and youthful children in the areas. Apparently, however, notable builders around the nation were itching for the opportunity to begin working with Bernard on his plan.

As soon as the man saw this, he was not surprised to see the name that appeared in the next paragraph of the article. Jude Falco was a name that the man had seen all too often in his career as an architect. Jude graduated from the same school that the man did, and always seemed to be a thorn in the man's side when trying to capture projects in the area. Whenever the man was able to lock up a lucrative job, Jude was always in the mix. Fortunately, Jude always seemed to be a step slower than the man. Of course, Jude would be itching for the opportunity to surpass the man's architectural resume without even thinking of the negative outcomes that the job may bring.

The article explained that Jude matched up with Bernard very recently and was eager to get started building. Jude was no slouch by any means in the business. He was able to get many of the projects that the man did not want. Some of his greatest accomplishments were listed in the paper, namely, a building that sported an extremely large fish tank around its exterior. The man scoffed at the mention of this "phenomenon" of a build, having full faith that the fishy design would go wrong in a short matter of time. The man supposed that it was inevitable for Bernard and Jude to meet once the man failed to contact Bernard after their meeting. Jude always seemed to have a decent read on jobs that the man was able to find, sniffing behind like a hyena ready to scavenge what the man did not want.

Things were starting to make sense to the man. It was no secret that many builders in the city were looking to do something with the beautiful outskirts of town. When this Bernard character came with a proven method to making money, it was only a matter of time before the idea was approved by the town. From what the man knew about the city's plot approval board, money was the driving factor in most land decisions. As long as builders could show the profitability of a business, ideas would be accepted far quicker than a more theoretical concept for the area.

Still, the man was suspicious of how the board of directors concluded on an idea like Bernard's so quickly. The man knew many of the board members, most of whom were raising young families in and around the city. Surely, they would have thought twice about bringing this project so close to their young ones. Bernard and Jude must have come to the board with numbers far greater than the city had seen in a long while. To pass this quickly, the city must have been given an offer that was too good to refuse.

Finally, the man reached into the depths of his mind to try and figure out what he could do to stop Bernard and his plan to bring a bounty of brothels so close to his home. The man had a long history with the city's board of directors, he thought perhaps they would be willing to listen to him if he came to them with a separate profitable idea for the patch of land. Alas, he did not have anything specific to bring to the board's attention, given that he had missed his appointment with the scholars. He could try to reason with Jude, but the man knew that would be a lost cause from the outset. Jude made it very clear on several occasions that he was furious whenever he played second fiddle to the man's heroic achievements within the industry.

It was never for a lack of trying. Jude seemed to work tirelessly day and night to spite the man and get the upper hand in their battles. There was a time where Jude found out the man had plans to use a city block to create a large-scale luxury apartment building. This was something that the city desired greatly, as it was trying to grow rapidly in population and wanted to offer convenient city living. Hearing word of this, Jude decided that he had to do something quickly and threatened to use his own savings to fund a gymnasium to put in the lot instead. Unfortunately for Jude, the city board promptly decided to go with the greater need and approve the man's apartment building. The occasion showed the lengths that Jude was willing to go to dethrone the man, which he failed to do countless times.

The man thought he could try to reach out to the scholars again and set up a meeting to atone for his absence from the meeting prior. Unfortunately, this seemed a bit of a long shot with them already letting the man know they were headed in a different direction. In the end, perhaps the promise of money in the brothels was too much to withstand, even for the man.

The man put down his phone and blankly stared into the open as thoughts continued to swirl. It was very atypical for him to drop the ball like this, especially in an area which he cared deeply for. To the core of his stomach, he felt a rotten strike of lightning within himself. He could not find it in him to forgive himself for the damage that he would be bringing to the city and people around him. For as long as Bernard's kingdom would stand, the man would constantly berate himself for failing to do everything he could to stop the plague.

Quickly, the front door opened as the woman stormed into the house dripping with wetness. "It's pouring out there!" she yelled as she came inside and quickly disrobed her soaking garments. The man hardly caught a glimpse of her as she trotted up the stairs in her waterlogged running shoes. He could barely hear the squeaks of her soles drifting against the clean base of the hardwood steps. Once again, the man was deep within the hollows of his own mind, thinking of what he had done wrong and the decision he would have to make shortly.

Collapse

A few days passed since the man discovered that Bernard would be going forward with his plot. The man was hardly able to think, with a brutal mixture of being supremely angry with himself over the missed opportunity, combined with the looming threat of his offspring murdering millions. He found himself drifting so deeply into the depths of his own insanity that he could no longer bear to do anything work related.

The woman was so happy with how life was going that she hardly noticed a change in the man. She would leave for work in the morning and come back in the evening. It was only until recently when she gathered that her morning coffee was a bit colder and her evening meal a bit sparser. Still, she thought nothing of it and continued in her cheerful ways. She continued to get involved with her sisters. The group set their sights on planning trips they would all take once they all had children. Mountains one year, beach the next, anticipation was building throughout the family as they awaited the heavily anticipated birth of the couple's child.

The man's parents, too, were brimming with excitement at the idea of holding their grandchild for the first time. They constantly called to check on how the woman was getting along, and they were quick to offer any help needed. They also became quite invested in figuring out the sex of the child and what the name should be. Many times, they urged the woman to go back to the doctor to discover what the gender would be, but the woman assured them that it was still too early to tell. Further, she had always shown a liking to surprises and so she was not keen on figuring out the gender of the baby until they were born. For the couple, this meant that they had not spent much time discussing potential names for their child.

The woman's coworkers were getting ready to be without her again while she would go on maternity leave. Although the woman had been working harder than ever and promised that she would not be taking too much time away during her pregnancy, her coworkers still knew she would be gone for a while. As a new mother, the woman did not fully realize the time-consuming nature of the endeavor she was about to embark on. The coworkers were disheartened about the prospects of her absence because they felt they had just gotten her back after her time away. Still, they were very happy for the woman and could not wait for a time when she would bring her child into the office to meet the team. Already, they were wondering which kind of décor the woman would be putting up in the child's room. They remembered the woman's magic touch and were certain that whatever she went with would start a trend for new parents in the area.

Regarding where the new child would be staying, the couple had not yet put serious thought into the idea. They would have no trouble finding a room for the child in their large house. There were many rooms that both had not gone into for weeks, far more rooms than were needed for just the two of them. When they moved into the house, they had plans for all the rooms, however, they ended up spending most of their time in only a few locations. They found that they were able to enjoy any space in the house, no matter how small, as long as they were together. For the baby's room, the two seemed to still be in a bit of shock and surprise over the fact that they were with child and thus were not planning that far ahead.

As it seemed, all was going swimmingly, as the quiet house seemed to rest on a weekday afternoon. The appliances and lights were turned off. Soft rain drops drizzled against the porch and dripped down the tall trees in the backyard. There were even a few birds chirping in the distance. The streets outside the house were calm up and down, with the neighboring homes' occupants either inside working on their personal computers or out visiting the office. The woman was at work for the day. The only one who remained in the house was the man, who was sitting in his chair swinging back and forth with a maniacal grin plastered to his face.

This was not the grin of a man who was cheerful and delighted at the direction in which his life was going. Rather, this was the grin of a man who was no longer in control of his mind, and, increasingly, his bodily functions. In fact, for the life of him, he would not be grinning if he remembered how to control his facial muscles. Instead, he was deep in a cycle of thought within his own mind. He no longer existed within his body. He would not be able to feel even a bony punch to his arm. The sole sensations he could feel were his emotions turning over again like an ocean current deep within a trench.

His stare forward into the smooth wooden bookshelves extended for a marathon's distance. Someone could have walked into the room and sat down at the desk right across from him, and he would have no idea. This was a man who was questioning his very existence on the earth he had lived upon for so long. A man that felt he was dropping out of the profession that he had ruled for so long. He could not live with the failure that would inevitably be the result of his mishaps. His thoughts were flickering like an old tape brought out of the attic after years of collecting cobwebs and dust. He would try to control what was flashing within his mind, but he could not. He was simply an observer, as each passing thought slipped deep into the darkness.

While his thoughts flickered, one of them was of his future child going and visiting Bernard's kingdom which would be conveniently located so close to their home. He thought of the horrid things that would be going on there, and the kind of lessons that would be taught to his child. These were lessons of which the man would have no control over. He thought that perhaps this was the place where the child would turn into the beast of prophecy. A place where people are dehumanized, and the only goal being the pursuit of personal desires. How many unborn children would become the spawn of this dastardly venue?

The cauldron of the man's mind continued to swirl as thoughts fused into one another like a nebula. Slowly this concoction of thoughts began to slip further and further away from the man's consciousness. He was not aware that he had not taken a breath in over a minute, nor had he blinked. Seconds continued to pass as the blank stare continued. To an onlooker, there was no suggestion that an apocalypse of thought was occurring within the skull of this man.

Suddenly there was another glimpse. This time it was a vision of a figure that looked much like the man at a younger time. The young man stood amongst a field covered in human bodies strewn out across each other. The bodies were graying and buzzing with flies that landed endlessly upon the decaying flesh of the dead. There were sounds of moans coming from the field, as if it itself were slowly dying. Yellow grass sprung into flames in rows as the bodies began to catch aflame and the scent of burning skin spilled out into the air. Throughout the gruesome scene, the young man stood staring ahead with an enormous smile on his face. He seemed to enjoy standing tall as the world burned around him.

In an instant the man returned to the room gasping for air as he realized he had taken neither breath nor thought for well over a minute. He struggled as the new vision of what he assumed to be his future son burned into his mind. Like the deathly beast he saw before, he was struck to the nerve as he imagined looking deep into the eyes of the young man. He wondered if this was the future that the beast promised him would arrive. If the future were anything like what he had just seen, the man knew he needed to try and do what he could to stop time from unfolding in this manner. There was a speck of determination that returned to the man. If he could do one thing with his life, it would be to stop these visions from turning into reality.

The man was back to existence, but quickly he felt the pressure returning to him and his mind. He was scared to slip back into the unconscious state that he spent most of the morning in. How could one man deal with the pressure of being expected to save the world from imagined devastation? The man decided that sitting in his office would no longer do him, or the world, any good. He rose from his leather seat and gently walked over to the window.

Gazing outside, he could see the rain clustering in front of his view as it splattered against the glass mere inches from his face. He looked past these small rivers into the yard, which continued to change as the rain around him fell. There remained a quiet atmosphere to the place. Animals nestled inside their homes waiting for the storm to cease. The ground and the tall green grass never looked healthier, but it would soon turn to yellow if the onslaught of water continued for too long. The gray in the sky melted into the stringy loose clouds that hung over the earth. The wet road was glazed with bits of mud which hitched a ride on the tires of the neighbors' cars.

Finally, the man broke his gaze from the gray world and retreated into his office. He decided to walk around the house to try and alleviate his aching mind. Pacing back and forth through the kitchen and living room, he found that his mind continued to run faster than his feet were carrying him. He felt that he needed some sort of relief from the stress that he was feeling. It was then that he decided he must do something he had not done for some time.

His face sparked up as if he had just figured out the formula for some master equation which eluded mankind for centuries. Quickly, he made his way upstairs to his room where he threw on a yellow, fluorescent rain jacket and a hardly worn pair of boots. Anticipation filled his stomach as he descended the spiral staircase towards the garage. He got into his car and slowly turned to check for passersby as he pulled out into the muddy road. His clean tires greeted the mud skids and drifted by them as the man continued down the road towards town.

After about five minutes of driving down the darkened roadway, the man began to see shops and more signs of life around him. People were out and about on this dreary day, seemingly fed up with the seemingly constant rain that had been keeping them inside for the past months. Cars zoomed by left and right, but the man was focused on a mission to arrive at his final destination and would not be deterred. He felt as if he were a spacecraft pilot dodging through the countless bullets of an asteroid belt, high above the land which he inhabited.

Finally, the car pulled into a parking spot not far off the busy road. Tired from its journey, it was permitted to rest as the man turned off the engine. Outside there was a large sign that read "Hooligans Pub". The building the sign sat upon was a drab little place, sitting on a near empty lot without the prospect of inviting many explorers to enter. There were a few signs outside the venue which touted their ability to serve cold beer and appetizers. Many of these signs were poorly maintained, missing lights in essential areas of the design. It was not a large building, no bigger than a double wide trailer.

Slowly, the man opened his car door with caution as if he were the first person setting foot on another planet. He drew his legs out over the pavement at the pace of a clock's hour finger. Quietly, he lowered his body to the ground and got out of his car, shutting the door timidly behind him. He stood outside the vehicle and stared at the building as if in awe of such a dim sight. The place looked exactly the same as he remembered it.

While the man had been to this drafty pub many times before in his life, it had been ages since he was on its creaky wooden floors last. He stood outside remembering days when his father would bring him along for quick breaks throughout the workday. They would head in at differing hours of the day, depending on how the workflow was going at his father's craft shop. There was a special booth that they would sit at every time, nestled in the corner of the small place. The man's father would always get 2 pints of beer while the man, as a young child, would order chicken fingers. The man's father always emphasized how good the chicken fingers tasted, but really, he was just there to enjoy some beverages.

When the man grew up and stopped helping his father in the shop as often, their trips to the bar together started to grow further apart. The man's father would still go regularly, but it was not the same kind of visit without having his son there. He would simply sit by the bar and have a few pints before leaving. The man's father was a consistent drinker, but very seldom did he get drunk. Most of the time he would stop at a few pints.

In times of nostalgia, the man came to this bar and sat in that booth to order a few pints along with an order of chicken fingers. Occasionally he would try to get his father out for the event, but most of the time the two could not align their schedules for a visit together. Still, the man and his father would joke about their old times at this tiny place whenever they got to drinking together. During the last few years, the man did not have the will to get over to the bar while trying to figure out how to have a child. Thus, he expected the place to look a bit more worn down or even be torn from the ground when he arrived on this rainy day.

The man stood outside on the middle of this gray afternoon, staring at the pub from the parking lot. Eventually he remembered how to move forward and did so towards the puny door of the establishment. It was tucked in the corner of the building and would have been quite difficult to find had the man not been familiar with the place. As he walked through the door, he was greeted with the usual ring of a bell that was located just above the doorway. He entered the building and realized that it was not just the outside of this musty place that had not changed a bit.

The first place he looked to was that old corner where he and his father sat enough times to leave an imprint on the seats. Sure enough, it was still there as if a day had not passed since the last time the man saw it. The dull red pads that made up the benches were still worn and tattered, but sittable. The old wood of the table was still chipping, it needed to be sanded and refurnished years ago. It was a seat in the corner where no newcomer would ever consider sitting. The man would not have it any other way.

The man looked around the rest of the old bar. It all seemed to be the same as he remembered. There were still two tiny televisions that were displayed at the helm of the bar. The air hung with stale smoke which invaded the nostrils on each inhale. The perimeter of the wooden place was lined with posters and signed memorabilia that was the same as before. Some of the posters looked a bit more faded than in the past, but otherwise there was no indication that the bar existed in a present-day setting. The man found this to be a bit peculiar. He thought of how many other places in the area had changed their design as the years went on to keep up with the times. Televisions got bigger and more common, screens were placed at every table for ease of ordering, furniture was renovated to keep up with the style choices; not for this place. For as run down and forgotten as this bar was, it did stay true to its original form.

The man thought of some of the regulars that he had seen in his time at this place with his father. There always seemed to be a handful of commonplace characters that they would expect to see as soon as they walked through the tiny door. He could hardly remember their names, but the theme with most of them was common. They had all been regulars at the bar for years and they would keep coming back until they died. They disliked the new and flashy standard that other bars in town were trying to set. All they needed was a pint and a small 20-inch television to pass the time. They enjoyed each other's company. The man wondered if he would run into any of those ghosts of the bar's past. As he looked around, however, it seemed there was not a soul in sight.

That did not last long. The man looked down to the bar to see what kind of liquor they were serving these days. He was in the mood for just about anything at this point. He wanted to forget the rest of his life for a while. "One sec!" A voice came from the back of the bar area behind a set of rugged wooden double doors. The voice did not sound familiar to the man, who calmly waited for its owner to emerge.

Soon enough, a middle-aged red headed woman came through the double doors which were left swinging gently behind her. "We normally never get anyone at this hour, and I don't recognize you either. You must be new here. What can I get for you?" she chirped eager to serve the stranger in her bar.

"I haven't been here for years, but I used to come here often with my father when I was younger," the man responded. "Please get me a double bourbon on the rocks." With that the red-haired woman behind the counter quickly nodded and spun around to pick out a half empty bottle of bourbon. She swung the bottle down from the shelf and quickly tossed it into an old-fashioned whiskey glass with ice. She placed in firmly in front of the man.

"Well welcome back," said the red-haired woman. "I'm Debby. It's not often that I get an unfamiliar face around here. Makes sense that I haven't seen you though if you haven't been in for a while. I took over running this place about five years ago when my father passed away. He led operations here for over 30 years, so you must've crossed paths a time or two. So, what brings you back around, sir?"

"Yes, I believe I do remember your father when he was working here," the man pondered. "He was always friendly with the customers. Some of the regulars here seemed to regard him as family. He certainly created a memorable atmosphere within these walls, and I can see that has not changed a bit. I'm Joe by the way. I suppose I came back because I needed someplace to get away from it all for a bit. Had a troubled mind lately."

"Well, you've come to the right spot, Joe. Not many people come in here midday asking for double bourbons when everything in life is going dandy. Anyways, I won't prod into what's going on in your life. We've all got things we need to forget for a while. In fact, I think I'll pour up a drink and toast you to that Joe." Debby smiled as she poured herself a bourbon and clanked it against the man's glass before smoothly and delicately bringing it to her lips. Quickly, the brown liquid disappeared from her glass as she removed it from her mouth and lowered it back onto the wooden table.

Seeing that the man's glass was also empty, Debby continued, "In fact, that is such a nice proposition that this next one is on the house." She skillfully spun around the glass liquor bottle as she drained another double bourbon into the man's glass. The man smiled at her as he brought his glass up for another sip. He could feel himself loosening up as the burning liquid crept down his throat and became a source of warmness for the rest of his body. His tense mind started to alleviate, and he began to forget the reason he came to this old bar in the first place. For the first time in what felt like ages, the man was beginning to feel a sense of peace and restfulness in his mind.

As he continued to get settled in, he chugged down the second drink and promptly ordered another. It had been a long time since he had this many drinks. There were nights at home when he would retreat to the alcohol in his lonesome while he worried about how his wife and he were going to get through their troubles, but that would never be more than a glass or two. He thought back to his younger days in college where he could make it throughout the night drinking and then wake up to more. Those days were long past him. Now, he was already feeling heavily buzzed as he continued to sip. After the next drink was poured, he slowly made his way over to the booth where he and his father shared many memories.

He sat on the same right side of the booth that was always his. He looked towards the other side, the seat which his father always occupied. Already, his vision was getting hazy as he smiled and pictured his father as a younger man looking to him and asking him how the chicken fingers tasted. In front of the man's eyes, he saw the years pass as his father began to take on an older face with wrinkles growing and his hair becoming more colorless. As a child, he let the years slip by in a soundless current without noticing these fine details. Now, he painstakingly searched his past for special memories he had here with his father, down to the most miniscule detail.

Growing faintly in the background, the man started to notice songs beginning to play. He immediately recognized the first few that were played, as if the bar's playlist had not changed since those glorious days with his father. Drunk now, the man lunged from the booth and began dancing with glee to the sweet music that was coming from the low-quality speakers at this old shack. As he spun around and laughed, he caught a glimpse of Debby, whom he pointed at joyfully as he called for another round of bourbon. Any responsible bartender would have denied the man more beverages at this point, but there was something about the happiness he was showing at such simple aspects of life that urged Debby to pour up once more.

Things after that became very blurry. One second, the man blinked and looked down to see chicken fingers and fries. He thought he must have made a nostalgic order as he began to dig into the feast. The crispiness and decadence of the tenders and fries was unmatched by any other meal that he had eaten in his entire life. Another blink and he was looking at Debby and laughing while the bartender's face seemed to show signs of concern. "How are you getting out of here again Joe?" she questioned.

Another blink and the man was hunched over a small porcelain toilet in what he assumed was the pub bathroom. For all the times he had been here, this was a first. He threw up vigorously into the toilet and looked around. The graffiti-ridden stall was very narrow and smelled putrid. He looked down to his clothes which had caught some of his oral projectile on its way towards the white rimmed bowl. He could not see straight, with his head spinning around at the same speed as the brown water that was flushed down the toilet in front of him.

Next blink and the man was stumbling from the tiny bar, covering his eyes from the light as it was still midday when he emerged from the dark cavern. There were thin stretches of brightness breaking through the clouds and rain. He thought he could hear Debby saying something to him from behind, but he decided to continue regardless. He tripped and collapsed onto the hood of his car before sliding off onto the hot pavement. He closed his eyes again and next thing he knew he was buckled into his seat and the car was moving quickly with the road churning underneath it.

The car continued to zoom forward as the man could hardly see the wet ground disappearing below his line of sight. He was moving fast, far more dangerously than his usual driving pace. He acknowledged this fact as he pushed his foot against the gas pedal harder. The engine roared over the backdrop that the sound of raindrops made against the windshield. The wipers were moving to their fullest extent, but it was not enough to persuade the rain away from the man's clouded line of vision.

Suddenly, there was a pop and a jolt from one of the tires on the right side of the vehicle. The car went airborne and for a moment everything in the vicinity was suspended. The car hung midair in peace for a fleeting moment. Abruptly, there was the sound of wheels landing back on the ground and the body of the car lurching about. The car shook for a few seconds before settling back into its usual state. The man sat still in the driver's seat in an unconscious state. Rain pounded against the glass in front of him and the wipers ceased to part the sea of water.

It was a matter of minutes before the man started to blink rapidly and take a gasp as he woke. He shuddered, not remembering where he was or what was going on around him. He was reminded due to the faint beeping noise that came from his car. He wondered where he landed, but he could not see out the window due to the vigorous and constant stream of water. He slowly moved his body and to his surprise discovered no soreness in his legs or arms. At a snail's pace, he unbuckled his seatbelt and opened the car door to see where he had landed.

He stepped out of the car without his hood on, somehow forgetting the conditions of the outdoor world. As his hair quickly matted down in water, the man looked around in a full circle. It appeared that he had landed in an empty parking lot. He slowly turned to his right to see a large cathedral style building. Still foggy, he recognized the building as a church that he often drove by. The structure seemed to tower high above the clouds, past where the water droplets originated. It was made of giant gray stone and had carvings that appeared similar to the ancient castles that the man had heard stories of. The stone rooftops extended into sharply pointed peaks that pierced the gray sky. The few windows that the building had were on high floors and were too dark to see through into the interior. Rain dropped in small waterfalls from the corners of the building, which remained unaffected.

It was then that the man heard a crack of thunder and saw lightning strike eerily close to his car which remained humming in the parking lot. He was beginning to regain his thoughts and realized he could not get back into the car to drive home while still under the influence of many bourbons. As he heard more rumbling thunder, he decided to throw on his hood and make his way in a quickened shuffle over to the large wooden doors of the church in front of him. He prayed that the doors would be open to him at this hour.

The man reached out and grabbed the large steel handle on the rustic door and gave it a frightful tug as rain and lightning seemed to pour around him. He could have sworn he saw a bolt of lightning nearly approach him and tap him on the shoulder. The wind howled as the man's vision began to tunnel once more. Deliberately, he yanked the doors and gasped with thankfulness as the church opened itself to him. He quickly found himself surrounded by the warmth of the interior of the building. He dove through the doorway, leaving a puddle of water beneath him as he began to look around his new environment.

The place was lit only by a few candles, a yellow hue covering the entrance area. The man breathed the air, scented with a subtle tangy aroma. He got the feeling that the place was empty aside from himself. He pushed himself up with his arms extended and raised himself upright. Standing in the entrance of the church, he looked up towards the ceiling. It seemed as if endless, the height of the building was magnificent both inside and out. He could hardly see into the dark crevices that made up the roof's interior.

Once more, the man took a deep breath from the rich, slightly smoky air of the church. It had a crisp feel to it, as if no one had breathed this air in quite some time. He found it to be refreshing as he continued to sober up from the multitude of drinks he consumed. The air was vastly different from that which he was breathing from inside the stuffy bar. Each breath was deep and fulfilling to the lungs.

The man stepped forward into the church nave and saw long, well-finished wooden pews that extended wide across the central area. There were at least four pews on either side of him as he slowly walked down the center aisle. The man looked down as he continued towards the altar which shone with brilliance that emanated throughout the darkened halls of the church. The path that he walked along was a carpet red as blood. This material extended all throughout the breaks in the pews. He continued to survey the church, looking at portraits that hung on the walls to each side of the area. His pace slowed to almost a crawl as he soaked in the feeling of this place.

It had been a long time since he had felt this feeling or been within the halls of a church. As a young boy, he grew accustomed to going to Sunday mass regularly with his family. Rain or shine, he would always arrive at the gates with his mother and father ready to hear the fresh story that the priest would tell each week. At times it was hard for him to understand what was being said or the message that was being conveyed, but he still felt a sense of holy compassion whenever he walked out the gates to end mass.

When the man grew older, he began to stop attending church as regularly. He would not go while he was living on his own but would still make occasional visits whenever his family offered. Although his visits were not as consistent as they once were, he still felt that same feeling whenever he entered the halls of the church. The feeling was coursing through him as he continued down the aisle with a smile on his face.

Suddenly, the man realized that he did not come here for this holy feeling but instead to evade the storm that was thrashing the outside of the church. He was amazed at how readily the cherished feeling was able to enter his system unexpectedly and without invite. As he neared the altar, he remembered the struggles he was going through that brought him to this place. The alcohol he consumed did not give him an answer to his questions, and he figured he may try his hand at a different route.

The man looked straight ahead and realized he was right in front of the altar. He looked at the glowing golden table that stood tall in front of him. There was nothing on it besides a beige cloth which was draped along the ends of the table. He looked up and saw a huge cross hanging over the altar stage. It felt as if the mighty power of the symbolic monument was weighing down on him, while at the same time he felt weights lift from his shoulders. He stared into the cross a moment longer before retreating to the first row of pews.

Gently, he began to bring down the red cushioned tuffet so that he could go to his knees and begin to pray. This was a form of prayer that the man had not considered in a long time. Even when he attended church regularly, he would not kneel in this fashion. He felt as if he were a foreign presence as he placed his wobbly knees gently upon the scarlet cushion. He thought rapidly about what he should be doing at this very moment. Should he be internally speaking, or speaking out loud? What was it that he should be saying or thinking? Should he be asking for guidance or forgiveness?

He closed his eyes and finally he felt what he desired for so long, silence. There was not a sound coming from the wide halls of the church, even though the storm continued to lash out in all directions outside. The man felt as if his body was relieved of all the weight he was carrying. He could no longer feel his knees against the cushion beneath them, nor his elbows on the wooden stand in front of him. He could feel his lungs filling deeply with the clean purified air of the church. His eyes only saw the blackness of his eyelids as he slowly felt a smile creep onto his face. He began to feel so comfortable, worrying he may fall asleep, when suddenly he heard a small voice. His heart leapt at the idea that his questions may finally be answered with confidence.

"Hello," was all that the voice said. At once, he tried to answer with his own greeting from within his head. He thought the words and waited. "Hello," the voice beckoned him once more, imperceptive to the response from within the man's head. "Hello," rang in his ears once more. It was this third time that the man realized the voice was not calling to him from within his mind but instead seemed to be coming from the neighboring pew. He slowly looked that way and opened his eyes, completely oblivious to who or what he may encounter.

Sitting at the pew looking at him was a man. The man had long stringy dark brown hair and an untamed beard that hung well below his chin. He was slender and wore a baggy torn jacket with a stretched out white shirt underneath. His skin appeared to be stained a shade of gray as if he had not cleaned himself in quite some time. The raggedy man produced a gap-filled smile when he saw that the man had opened his eyes to see him. Despite the scruffy appearance of this newcomer, his eyes were a deep and youthful brown.

"I thought you'd fallen asleep. The rain is getting pretty bad out there, I often find it comforting to come in here and wait out the storms. This is one of the few places in town that I can always rely on to be open and quiet," said the man with few teeth. "Although I am glad that someone finally stumbled upon this place, it was getting frightening here all alone. I'm David, fellow traveler, nice to make your acquaintance. Did you come in here to pray or to escape the storm?"

"Hello David, my name is Joe," said the man with a half drunken smile. "I ran into a bit of a predicament and lost my ability to get home just as this storm came along. I hoped I could come in here and wait for the storm to pass. When I got into this place, though, I began to get the feeling there was more to do here besides wait for the rain to soften. The beauty of this place took control of me, and I started praying in a way I have not done in many years. At least, I believe that it was praying."

"That was a good idea, Joe," David replied. "I have said many prayers in my life, and they have all been answered. Despite my appearance and my homelessness, I have everything that I want from this world. I've found ways to create my own happiness without needing the luxuries that most people depend on. For instance, I've become quite joyful just by sparking up conversations with others like I have with you today. If you don't mind my asking, what was it that brought you here today and what were you praying for?"

The man took a breath before his answer, "Well I think you'd hardly believe me at all David. For starters, I recently found out that my wife and I are going to be having a child. This was after an arduous and emotionally draining process. I'm not sure that I'm ready for the struggles of raising a child. I have wished and dreamed about the great parts of being a father for so long, but my vision of the difficulties that would come with it was previously clouded."

"That is understandable Joe. I have never had the privilege of raising a child myself, but I do feel that I have raised the hopes of the many people I have met. In all aspects of life, it is hard to take the opening steps to begin a new journey. You are planning to enter a bond which you could not have conceived in your life to this point. Think, however, of how many people have done what you are about to do. Surely, it is possible, you seem like a capable man," David chuckled.

"I suppose that is true, many have been fathers before me, and many will continue that trend after me. Though, that is not the only thing that concerns me. I have been burdened with these premonitions which you are welcome not to believe. The theme of the messages has been that my child is going to do heinous things in the future, and I may be the only one able to stop them from occurring," the man continued.

"That is certainly enough of a vision to harm any man," replied David, "but have you considered that these thoughts may too be a result of your doubts in becoming a father? Why do you think your life is worth so much importance to this world that you will be the only one who can stop its imminent demise? It may be the case that many others before you have had these same visions, yet the general success of humanity leads me to believe that any hypothesized apocalypse has not yet come to fruition. Is your life so important to this universe that you alone will be able to restrain harm that comes from your own loins? How can you be sure that your life is not just another spoke in the wheel of time? Further, even if your child does set off on a track to cause this harm you speak of, is it impossible that someone else may come along to intervene?"

The man leaned his head back, contemplating what he was hearing from this man who looked to be one with the earth itself. "I suppose you are correct in saying that it is unreasonable for me to think that my life is of such importance that the world would convey such a responsibility upon me. When I recall these visions, however, they feel so real that I get the sense that the outcome may truly rest upon my shoulders. It may be insane to think such a thing under the circumstances, but this is the length to which these thoughts have driven my mind into the depths of insanity. As for someone else coming along to stop any future misfortune, the same answer applies. I was distinctly told that I was the only one who could stop what is to come. I have even seen visions of this future that rattle me to the bone. If I had a feeling that this crisis could be averted in any other way, surely my mind would not be constantly wrapped around the subject. The fact of the matter is that this vision of the future demands my complete attention."

David shifted in his seat as he continued, "Perhaps it is attention that you want from this wild tale which you speak. I wonder how many you have told about these stories, and what you may have to gain from spreading them. Surely, it is inconceivable that many people would believe you."

The man recoiled at this statement, "This is not something I've been going through for the attention, in fact, there is only one person I have told the story to in confidence. That was my therapist, who believed there was a possibility that the universe was trying to send me a message. Besides, I am not one for boasting or spreading fairy tales. I just wish for a happy life for my family. My name need not be spoken by the mouths of others, nor remembered in their minds."

"That is refreshing to hear in a world where so many are driven by an insatiable desire to be great," David smiled. "There are no limits to the lengths people will go in order to have their names written in the history books. I believe people generally begin wanting to be remembered for helping people or doing something of benefit to the world. If this does not work out, they will be driven to do anything simply to be remembered, even if it means performing evil actions. The inhabitants of this world have become too obsessed over what others think about them, to such an extent that they feel the need to be remembered by those they will never meet."

"I have been trying to make good decisions, but it seems like lately my attempts have been futile. Just recently I let myself become so distracted that I missed out on a job opportunity that could have positively impacted the youth of this town. I let my obsession drive me to blindness. As opportunity drifted from my fingertips, it gently fell into the waiting arms of another. I fear that what they are building out there could have repercussions that are felt far beyond our lives my friend," the man sighed.

"Build something? I recently came across a newspaper and read about the commission of a new entertainment plaza on the outskirts of the city. Those fields used to be a place I would visit regularly. They were serene, I was able to walk around with my hands drawn out by my sides brushing up against the tall vegetation in the field. I was upset to see that the fields would be destroyed in order for that brothel network to be built. I should have known that my paradise would not last out there. There is no money to be made from having an open field so close to a city bustling with people. Money rules this world, regardless of whether the motive behind it is pure or evil," David said as he drew his eyes towards the cross that hung above the altar.

"That is the same place that I speak of! I had the opportunity to build a school there that would give the youth a positive vision of the future. Although I did have better intentions for the area, I too wished to take away that field so that I could build something to bring people closer together. I am sorry that you will be losing that field, David."

"Oh, that's alright Joe. A traveler like myself will always be able to find another place where I can find peace, like the church in which we sit now. And do not be ashamed of the opportunity that you missed out on Joe; it was the promise of money that turned the fate of the field." David looked up towards the ceiling to see if he could see through any of the windows. "I haven't heard any thunder in quite some time. I would say the rain has lightened up to the point where I can get back on my way. It was great to meet you Joe, I hope that you're able to find the answers that you seek."

With that, David slowly rose from the pew he was sitting in and smiled towards the man, who gave a nod goodbye. The light from the altar shone on David as he slowly made his way down the center of the church towards the big doors at the end of the hall. The man continued to watch him for a moment before turning his head back towards the altar. He heard the loud creak as the doors to the church slowly opened and then shut. The man nodded his head forward, tired and wondering how he was going to get home.

Climb

For a moment it seemed as if the sun was considering shining as drops of rain trickled down the sloped roof of the house. There were birds chirping outside as they flew back and forth from the feeder to the tree line. Squirrels were making their way around the backyard, trying to scavenge food which they had scoped out while the rain was pouring down. The wetness on the roads was beginning to subside, and while it was still raining, it seemed that for the moment the worst of it had let up.

It had been around a month since the man took his trip to the bar. Fortunately, he never had to face the music for his actions on that day. He was able to sober himself up before long and drive back to his home. He was also lucky to hear that there was no substantial damage done to his vehicle, which he found out after taking his car into the auto shop in the city. For the time being, the man felt that he was on the ascent.

In his mind, he had braved through the eye of the storm and made it out alive. The torment which he agonized over for so long seemed as if it were a storm drifting off into the outskirts of sight's reach. After his time in the church, his mind felt as if it had changed courses like the flip of a switch. The man believed what David told him on that fateful day and was beginning to feel that the whole ordeal was nonsense stemming from the darkest corners of his mind.

While the man's visions from the early part of that day were cloudy and hazy, he had a vivid memory of what occurred within the church on the rainy afternoon. He could still elaborate mentally on the tiniest of details from his experience. From the large cross that hung suspended over the alter, to the bristles on David's furry face, the man felt that he could recite every vision and line that he encountered there that day.

There was nothing flashy about David or what he said to him, but it was just that which made the man believe the sentiments even more. David did not try to sell the man on any truths, he was not conversing for personal gain like Dr. Lucas or Bernard. There was no motive for their conversation, it was simply the reciting of the man's tale to David regarding what he had encountered during the previous months. To a disinterested party, it was clear that the man's story was crafted through the torment he had sown within his own mind. Even Marcus, who was hired by the man, may have had an ulterior motive in having the man come back to see him in need of a therapist.

In a calming sense, the man began to smile and laugh at the lengths he went to in order to try and figure out the solution to a problem that he did not have. Long days focused on research trying to find answers, going out of his way to talk with a professional, and stirring his mind constantly to figure out what needed to be done. In the end, he determined that floating down the river of life suited him better than constantly berating himself in an effort to control his future and that of those around him.

Still, there were times when the memory of that darkened beast would rear its soulless face towards him, but he was succeeding more at turning his view towards brighter futures. No longer would he allow himself to fixate on the fictions that his mind had furnished. He reasoned that these visions were manifested from the doubts that he had about becoming a father. For all the time he had spent obsessing over the decision he thought he would make, it seemed that the answer appeared to him in an instant. The man was deciding to let things fall as they would, he would not tell his wife that she would have to abandon their child in fear of them one day becoming a monster. He would not let his parents down by informing them that they would be going on without a grandchild. He began to wish once again for the days of seeing the joy light up all of their faces as they stared down into the eyes of the new being.

Things were starting to look much more joyful around the house and at work as well. The man was finding ways to keep his mind more focused on the tasks of the day and those around him. The woman was beginning to show signs of pregnancy with a tiny lump protruding from her stomach. The two laughed with glee when they finally had to decide whether this was from a child within her, or if she had eaten too much the night before. One thing was apparent, the family was beginning to form itself around the child that was growing within the woman.

Work was beginning to pick up for the two of them as well. The woman finally decided to undertake the task of designing the room that would be their child's. She worked tirelessly night and day to find the best ideas and schemes for a children's room. She looked for the finest colors to facilitate a learning mind, and the optimal cribs for deep sleep. At work, she shared what she was learning with her customers and coworkers and was fast to begin setting up a new line of merchandise fit for a newborn child.

The man, too, was finding more work than he had in the months prior. Finally, he felt as if he could place his attentive focus on his job once again. Without his head spinning, he was able to connect deeper with his clients and his team. New calls with exciting opportunities were passing through his office almost daily. The team was even able to find an opportunity to create a building near the fields on the outskirts of town. These were not the fields the man originally hoped to build in, but they would do, nonetheless. "They want a flower!" was the last thing the man could remember from his conversation with his team as he sat silently in his home office gazing out into the drizzling morning.

It was a peaceful day; rain gently fell outside while the man and woman worked. Both wore smiles for most of the day, and although they could not see each other, they could feel that the other was radiating the same joy that they felt. Peeking through the clouds, they could feel the sun's warmth on their faces as they stepped outside to enjoy the day.

In the evening, the man had a magnificent feast prepared for the woman right as she came through the door to their home. He greeted her with a kiss as she slipped off her shoes and proceeded to the kitchen, marveling at how delicious it smelled. The man prepared a brown bean stew that was still bubbling with anticipation on the stove. There was lamb which was well seasoned with a generous portion of herbs and spices. Plump green olives sat in a bowl that awaited the rest of the feast on the table. Also, on the table sat a savory crab dip that would go well with the toasted garlic bread that accompanied it. Finally, in the corner of the table sat a fine Italian wine with some dates scattered around the base. The table was so full of food that the man and woman pulled their chairs together on the same side and salivated as they looked on in anticipation.

They looked at each other and smiled with a knowing nod of approval as they each gave themselves permission to dig in. The night was a blur from there on. The man and woman had an enchanting evening chewing and laughing constantly throughout the night. Conversation was flowing like sand down the hourglass of time. It mattered not what they were talking about, all that mattered was the love they shared for one another glowing radiantly in that moment. When they finally came down from the high, they looked to the clock which had crept past midnight. It was time for them to rest, and they were both able to sleep soundly throughout the dark rainy night.

The two woke at precisely the same time the next morning, both grinning widely as they turned to look at each other. They were thrilled to be able to spend another day relaxing to themselves. After some time discussing the musings of the week and plans for the distant future, they began to talk more seriously about the child that would be arriving.

The first order of business was finding a room for their child. Luckily, there was a cozy little room right by their bedroom that would serve well. It was a room they had not used in many years, a place where they would put old technology of the past. When new technology came out, the two were quick to purchase it despite not being quite ready to part with their old devices. Having more rooms than they knew what to do with, this small room somehow became designated as the room for misfit devices.

With the child in mind, however, both the man and woman were quick to conclude that they would be delighted to get rid of the old tech for the opportunity to have their child sleep so close to them. Although the room was petite, it would make for quite a child's room. It had a wide doorway which would be easy to fit the crib through and be safe to stumble through in the night whenever the child called. There was also a small window overlooking the backyard which would give the child a glimpse into the open world while the parents were away. The room also was not painted in any color, nor was there much on the walls, so it would be easy to overhaul the area and make it into a worthy home for a loved child.

Next came a topic that the two had been putting off for a long while. They needed to decide on a name for the baby. "Alright, we've both had enough time to brainstorm, years in fact," the woman said with a wry smile. "I think it's about time we gave our kid a name." The man agreed. He lamented that during his days of worry, he neglected to think of what they should call their child. Giving the child a name would bring a sense of life into his unborn offspring and bring them a step closer to birth.

This led to the two sitting comfortably in cloth loungewear and scrolling their phones looking for ideas for child names. They decided they did not feel the need to name their child after a family member from the past, as is often the case in families. Instead, they wanted to have the name be one of their own creation and volition. Quickly, they realized that they did not know the sex of the child, making name creation a difficult task. "The anticipation is wearing on me. I wanted to wait, but I'm too excited. We should go back to the hospital and get them to check to see if we will have a boy or a girl," the woman commented with a grin.

With that, the man quickly searched the internet for the Pear Tree Hospital to get the number to call and set up an appointment. He scrolled through the results, puzzled that he could not find the hospital. After a few more searches of hospitals in the area, the man started to become agitated that there was no sign of the Pear Tree Hospital online. "I'm not sure why I can't find this place on here. I swear I remember looking through the posts from their past patients on their website. There was a picture of the building and Dr. Lucas on there and everything."

"That's ridiculous," said the woman. "How could a place up and disappear just like that? Now that I think about it, it is strange that we haven't heard from the doctor or anyone at the hospital in a matter of months. Surely, we can get a hold of them, call their numbers. If that doesn't work, we'll take a ride down there and see what the deal is."

With that, the pair began frantically looking through their old call history and contacts trying to find a way to contact this elusive establishment. The man called the number that he had saved as Dr. Lucas. As he called on speaker phone, the couple held their collective breath as they started to worry about what may have happened to their hospital. The phone shook in the man's palm when they heard the distinctive triple tone of a number that was not connected. The woman tried another number from the hospital that gave them the same result. The two looked at each other with confusion and despair on their faces.

The man jumped up and began looking for the bright red letter that started them down this journey. He distinctly remembered that the letter contained the contact information, specifically the address of the hospital. He ran into his office and flung papers from his desk in search of the note. After a few minutes of searching, he hung his head in defeat and returned to the woman empty handed. Looking equally defeated, the woman's eyes told the man that she was no more successful in her search for the letter.

"Alright, well this is just a bit of a snag. Let's drive over to the hospital and I'm sure they will explain this away easily. Perhaps they changed their internet address and their phone numbers," the woman said as hope began to drain.

With that, the man and woman found themselves driving down the long road outside of their neighborhood while the rain pounded against the windshield. The wipers toiled vigorously to try to clear the path for the man to see while the car slowly tumbled down the pavement. The couple was certain that they remembered the way to the hospital, it had been right around the corner from their house. When they needed to decide which street to turn down, however, they found it difficult to recall. It turned out their thoughts were scrambled with doubt and hope when they first made the trek out to the place.

After a long while of stressful twists and turns through side streets, they finally were able to roll up to a building that looked familiar to them as the hospital. The man slowly brought the car up to the curb by the entrance of the decrepit gray building. Through the rain, they could not see any signage or lights to suggest that this was a running hospital. In fact, there was no sign that this building had ever been a hospital at all. The two turned towards each other once more with even more stunned worry.

At once, the man jumped out of the car and was immediately drenched with rain which seemed to pour down harder as he sprinted his way to the entrance of the abandoned building. He saw the glass panels that he remembered and pounded away at them with thuds that could not be heard over the storm above. He cupped his hands over the glass to create a glimpse through the water which was streaming down the glass almost unfettered. Through his wet hands, he could see nothing in the interior of the building but a cleared space. Nowhere to be found were the welcoming desks nor rows of chairs that he remembered so vividly.

The man slumped his wet shoulders until they hit the puddles on the ground in front of him. Slowly, he made his way back to the car where his wife sat with her face deep within the palms of her hands. He could see that there were tears rolling down her face as she wept silently.

"I'm not sure what's going on," he began, "but this does not take away from the journey we are embarking on. You are showing signs of pregnancy, I am certain that there is a child growing within you. We do not need a hospital and the assistance of doctors to be sure that this is happening for us."

The woman brought her head from her damp palms slowly and looked at the man with reddened eyes.

"We've learned that we can't base our hope off the words of doctors nor in science, look where it has led us. Instead, I will believe in our love and choose to put aside any doubts I've had about our ability to have this child. I have a feeling our child is a boy; we will name him James."

The man nodded.

Birth

The following several months after the night in the rainy parking lot flew by like a dove soaring through the sky with a twig held tightly in its beak. The couple was able to drive home together that night with valiant confidence despite the fact that the foundations of their world were seemingly crumbling around them. There was no more questioning what happened to the Pear Tree Hospital or the people that the couple encountered during their time there. There was no second thought to the idea that the two were going to be parents in the very near future. About this, they were certain, and they did not need any external affirmation to know what lay ahead.

This newfound clarity brought peace to the couple and those around them. Evenings once more became filled with laughter as the man and woman danced around their future child's room, getting it ready for its occupant. The woman and her sisters were talking regularly on the phone and were starting to book trips together for when the woman's pregnancy came to an end. The man's parents, too, were coming over more often than ever before to share their newest findings in their research seeking ways to have the healthiest and longest living child imaginable.

The house itself was consistently filled with light. It seemed to be personifying the joy that was displayed by the family at the thought of their future member growing steadily. The lit rooms served as a beacon for those walking through the rainy outdoors to arrive at the calm and peaceful house. Within the walls, there was constant chatter about what goodness the arrival of the child would bring. It was as if the walls themselves were talking.

It was late in the year when the family met at the house for a Saturday afternoon brunch. The man's parents trudged through the front door around noon and sloshed off their boots and raincoats to hang and dry. With a hearty laugh, the elders announced their presence and delivered hugs to the man and the very pregnant woman. The quartet could not help but smile as they walked back to the kitchen to begin what was going to be an eventful day.

At this point, the woman was deep in her pregnancy and thus off cooking duty, not doing much moving around at all. She lounged deeply in a fluffy cushioned chair which sat in the family room of the home. The man and his parents sat around her in chairs of their own as they continued their greeting and began to talk about life.

They talked about how their days were going and what they were excited for in the future. The man's parents were at a point in their lives where they were not quite working, but still trying to remain busy. The woman was still satisfied with how her work was going. She finished up a brilliant design for a child's room that was the same one that adorned the small room upstairs in her house. The design was placed at the front of the store so that all customers could enjoy it immediately upon entry. She continued to work up to this point in her pregnancy, even being so close to giving birth. Her coworkers continuously praised her for her dedication to the job despite the load she carried in her stomach.

The man was happy with how his job was going as well. He continued to find work and was successful in forgetting his failures of the past. He met frequently with his team and felt that morale around the office was at an all-time high. His team all shared their excitement for the man about to become a father.

They talked about the state of the world and how they saw it. All of them were up to date on the latest musings of the national news and were eager to talk about the hot topics. They were not divisive in their opinions, rather just interested to hear that others had read the same information. There was nothing too drastic going on around the world at this time, just billions of people finding things to talk about.

Next, they all took a walk up to see the baby's room. The man and woman did not tell anyone what they planned to call their child. They did not want to cause alarm when others found out that they had only picked a name for a boy. Their premonition that they knew the sex of their child without going to the doctor first would have people laughing. Instead, the family would just have to wait and see if they had a boy or girl, and they were extremely eager.

The man's parents looked for clues when they came into the breathtaking room that the woman spent so many hours designing. The walls were dressed in a violet shade that soothed the mind and brought thoughts of enjoying buttery blueberry pancakes out by the water's edge. The wispy white curtains hung perfectly to the tip of the ground which was a cedar hardwood cut perfectly in grain. They gently swayed with the wind that entered through the small window which was cracked open. The crib was the centerpiece of the room and had the most unique characteristics. It stood low to the floor and was made from brilliant red sandstone. What the crib lacked in softness, it made up for in strength to hold the child tirelessly.

In the corner of the room stood a dresser made of fine mahogany wood that the man's father noticed immediately. He recognized it as one of the first items he and his son worked on in the shop. They made it years ago for the man to have somewhere to put his clothes. When the young man suggested they go to the store and buy a dresser, the man's father responded that it was always more fulfilling to get the job done your own way. To this day, the shelves of the dresser maneuvered flawlessly, without a creak. The man's father looked to the man and woman and smiled at them both.

The family then made their descent back down the spiral stairs to the living room where they sat slowly and looked at each other happily. It appeared to them that at this very moment all was well in the world around them. They wished for time to stand still enough for each to take a collective breath without thinking of how the future would go. They did not want to worry about the direction in which their lives would take. They did not want to think about how fast the roller coaster of life would begin to vault them as soon as the happiness of having this child engulfed their lives. For the moment, there was a serene peace amidst the rain.

Suddenly, the woman jolted in pain and let out a brief gasp that broke the silence around her. The group collectively blinked and focused in on her as they saw her begin to topple over in pain. "It's happening!" the woman yelled as she began to lay her hand flat on the floor to stop herself from falling over completely. With that, the rest of the family snapped into motion, quickly jumping towards the woman to lift her back to her feet. As the man's mother and father gathered the woman up in their arms, the man leapt to the kitchen to grab his car keys.

Within moments and without a word, the family was making their way into the garage down worn steps with the man zooming ahead of the group to open the back seat for the woman to get in. He flung open the door and in went the woman slowly and carefully as she gasped out once more in pain. The man's mother followed the woman into the back seat, the woman squeezing her hand with a cobra like grip. The man looked into the woman's eyes as sweat dripped down her face and he closed the door behind his mother. In a single bound, he sprang around to the driver's seat of the car as his father got in on the passenger side.

In an instant, they were speeding down the road just as the rain quickened and thunder started to grumble overhead. In the distance, they could see flashes of lightning coiling in thick streaks through the clouds. As if by the second, the rain began to fall harder as it buffeted against the vehicle like gunshots. The street was quickly soaked in water as oceans rushed swiftly towards the storm drains. Soon, there was thunder crashing all around them and they could no longer hear the wails of the woman in the back as she dealt with the pains of childbirth.

Through the storm, the man continued to drive the car forward towards the nearest hospital. Were it that Pear Tree was still up and running, it would have been a much shorter drive. Instead, the voyage was going to take them the better part of an hour in the rain that crashed around them. The man was maneuvering the car as fast as it could go while still retaining friction with the road. His foot was slammed against the gas pedal like a boulder, and he could feel the tires starting to lose their grip on the slippery road. He cursed the rain that felt the need to drop so harshly at a time when the group needed it least.

The man and his father sat staring ahead at the road. The car had reached its limit and there was nothing more that could be done as the woman curled up in pain. The man's mother sat in the back with her, consoling and allowing the woman to squeeze her until her circulation was cut off. Outside of the cries from the woman and the sky, not a word was uttered for the remainder of the trip. After what felt like centuries, the car finally pulled into the hospital and splashed to a stop in front of the building.

Waves of water erupted around the car as the tires attempted to screech to a halt. Any passerby on this ill day would have been soaked to the bone if they were standing too close. Fortunately, not a soul was thinking about going outside and braving this treacherous terrain. In a flash, though, three of the car doors simultaneously flew open. The only one remaining shut was the one on the side that the woman was nearest to. The man jumped out and ran around the back of the car where he was greeted by his mother and father as they were pulling the woman gently out to the curb. As instantaneously as the car doors had opened, they were all rapidly drenched with water and looked as if they had walked out of the sea.

To no avail, they attempted to use their clothing to cover up the woman as they hastily walked to the double doors of the hospital. The water seemed to flow straight through the clothes and right onto the woman's head as she shivered through clenched teeth. The walk to the door occurred within a few seconds, but to the group it felt as if they were walking a marathon. When they finally arrived at the pearly gates of the hospital, they were relieved that the doors automatically flew open as if greeting them with hearty emotion.

Unprepared and unknowing that a pregnant woman was walking through the door of the hospital, the few workers who were in the area stopped and stared at the wet bunch as they made their way into the dryness of the building. They were well trained, however, and it took only a moment and a glance at the woman, with her full stomach and ferocious cry, to realize that she was in the process of having a child. A gray-haired elderly woman from the crew snapped to first, and grabbed a rolling chair to put the woman in. In the background, the family could hear the muffled tone of another one of the workers calling for an emergency pregnancy. The next minutes were a blur, and the result was the woman being rolled down the long well-lit corridor of the hospital.

The man and his parents looked onward down the hallways at the woman being rolled away as she screamed. Their eyes were dilated as their view of the hallway closed behind white swinging double doors. They could still hear the woman wailing for a few more moments before the sound drifted away into the recesses of the hospital. It was only after an extended moment standing there dripping before they looked at one another and remembered to breathe.

They looked around the place they were standing in as if they had not noticed it on the way in. They made eye contact with the nurses who smiled at them and prompted them to take seats in the waiting area. Over in the corner of the hospital, by the tall glass windows dressed in water, were rows of chairs lined with a speckled blue fabric. Slowly, the family came to their senses and made their way over to a trio of seats stationed right next to the windows.

The group sat silently for a while, still collecting their thoughts after the hectic events that led them to this moment. Periodically, the nurses would come over and offer words of encouragement and tell them where the cafeteria was. None of the family members felt hungry, they were full of anticipation. Their stomachs were full of butterflies at the thought that the moment they dreamed of was finally happening. They could not help but wonder exactly what the child would look like upon first glance.

Inevitably, as they sat still, their minds began to drift towards the potential negative outcomes. Of course, they all had heard stories about tough child births, and it was clear that the woman was in immense pain and suffering the last they had seen her. As if they were reading each other's minds, they reached their hands towards one another and began to talk about the journey they went through to get to this moment. There were laughs, there were tears, and time passed gently as the group kept their minds occupied.

After a lengthy chat with his parents about more plans for the child's arrival, the man looked out the window. He could hardly see through the rain that was pounding against the glass so hard that he felt the need to pull his face back from the area. He saw that his car was still parked in the hospital driveway which was steadily being overrun with water. Thunder clashed in the pitch-black clouds over the place as he stared upward into the sparks of faint blue lightning. Despite the treacherous conditions of the day, the man searched for reasons to smile.

It readily came to his face as he thought about the voyage that he and his wife took to get to where they were. The rocky beginnings, the failed attempts to conceive a child, and concern whether their relationship would be able to survive the fissure that opened between them. The months of repulsion that ensued once they had all but given up hope. The seed of hope that then germinated in what they presumed to be a barren field of despair. The hesitant joy that they began to embrace when they found out they were going to be parents.

He thought back to that night in the yard, the vision. He thought that he would rather not recall in his mind the way that beast glistened in the night sky, nor the words that he heard it spew on that fateful night. Nor did he wish to contemplate over the months he spent searching for answers to what he had seen. The trips to professionals, the agony laced hours that he spent bashing himself for missed opportunities, and the countless drinks he poured up in an attempt to cope.

Then he settled upon thoughts of the future. Thinking up ideas of how he would help to raise his child to be a beneficial member of society. He hoped that his child would never worry about where to sleep or where their next meal was going to come from. This got him thinking about people in the world who had the fate of David, walking around without much evident purpose but still managing to bring light into the lives of others. The man gave silent thanks to those who had helped him on his journey. He sat in the chair looking out into the rainy abyss for a while, reminiscing while also excited for what the future would bring.

Next thing the man knew, he was being shaken awake by his parents who were watching intently as a doctor approached them with a cool and simple walk. The doctor was a short man with glasses and a stubbled beard, his nametag read Dr. Nolan. He approached the family gently, "You all are the Francis family, I take it. Thank you for waiting patiently out here while we worked with Meredith. She said that your name is Joe, would you like to come and meet your son?"

The next second felt like a generation as overwhelming joy filled the hearts of the collective family sitting in that pristine hospital lobby. Tears welled up in their eyes as they struggled to get out any word in response to this welcome messenger. Rather than speak, they all vigorously nodded their heads and grabbed at each other in a loving embrace. They got up and followed the doctor back through the double doors which opened into long well-lit hospital hallways. They knew not which route they took, but they were all as present as they had ever been in their entire lives as the doctor welcomed them into room 767.

They heard the child before they saw him, and their eyes quickly darted to the source of the high-pitched cry that the newborn was emitting as he lay softly in his mother's arms.

He was tiny, with his walnut sized hands nestled delicately against his mother's heaving stomach. His hair was dark and matted against his tiny pink forehead. For a moment, he opened his eyes to reveal a dense cocoa brown color. His tiny feet were attached to toes that were the size of peas. His weeping continued as the entire room continued to gaze at him in awe.

Rain chanted against the window as the family converged around the woman who sat smiling in her hospital bed. They laughed and cried as they all got a turn to hold the newborn boy. It was not every day that they got the chance to welcome someone new into the world, and it was a moment they waited for their whole lives. When the child was passed onto the man, he looked deeply into his son's dark brown eyes and said, "Hello, James."

The treacherous gray sky loomed over the hospital as thunder began to howl through the clouds like a wolf in search of prey. At the side of the hospital building there sat a crushed white egg. A life ended before the creature inside ever had the chance to inhale a first breath of air into its lungs. The rain gushed and flooded onward as the remains of the small egg were flushed into a nearby storm drain along with the cries from the heavens.

Reign

Showers draped their way downwards in a gentle fall towards the earth. Like a soft blanket, the drops quietly descended through the atmosphere. They politely glanced off mountains, trees, and blades of grass before they reunited with their watery colleagues atop the soil. The chorus of drops filled the air with a beautiful serenity that was invited to linger for as long as it wished. Water drifted over the hills and cleansed the land, trying to assist the soil in growing the crops that had long since vanished.

The air was quiet besides the patter of the water droplets hitting the terrain. Nary a sound could be heard as the warm washing water dissipated any outside noises. It was the kind of scene in which one could sit calmly for hours, meditating as the rain softly floated around them. The clouds in the sky were puffy and off-white. They elegantly graced the land with their presence as they drifted across the open sky. Along with the clouds came their welcoming shadows which covered the land from the harmful rays of the sun which had scorched the earth for some time.

There was no sign of people nor animals out on the open plains. Many of the buildings were wearing down at the foundations. The relics of the past were sinking into the earth as quickly as the delicate water that fell around them. Not much life traversed these lands, but the rain kept the land alive. A constant security, the rain could always be depended on to continue falling from the sky. It had been that way for a long time. The people who still inhabited the area could not remember the last time they had encountered a dry day. It was the life to which they had grown accustomed.

The people who still lived within the remains of the land learned to thank the rain for what it gave them. For many years, the elders remembered the fires that would burn vibrantly and destroy the things which they loved most. It was the rain that kept this destruction in check, the fires could never be permanent due to the quenching ability of the water. The water cleaned them when they lost the ability to bathe and could no longer find water sources that had not been contaminated. The water gave them one constant thing to look for in lives that were subject to changing within any hour of the day. Seeing the rain persist gave some of the people hope that they too would be able to endure as long.

Those who remained often looked up into the sky while it rained and braced for the worst. The lucky ones, if one could call them that, would be able to recall the days in which they looked out into the darkness as fireballs descended upon their homes. Like comets in the night sky, the fire danced towards the people and their loved ones in an unflinching motion. There was hardly any time for those on the ground to react to what was happening. Within moments of catching a glimpse of the soaring flame, structures which had been standing for decades collapsed to the ground in mere instants.

Families that were carefully constructed with love and care for many years crashed and burned to ashes in a matter of seconds. The scariest part for those who could remember was that there was no warning of what was coming. It all happened within a few hours on a day that seemed otherwise predictable and routine. It was hard for those who were born after that time to get the elders to speak about what they remembered about life before.

There were not many humans left for the rain to fall upon. The purge of humanity was unlike anything the world had ever seen before. The few that remained found refuge in the hollows of the earth, in the remnants of destroyed buildings, or simply laid out on the barren pathways that used to be bustling roads. For those that survived the initial onslaught, this life was shallow compared to the ones they lived in a past life. They learned to forget their joyous memories, knowing that no such emotion could ever find its way to them again. The luxuries which some of them enjoyed were no longer. Bars of soap were replaced with gravelly rainwater if one was fortunate enough to stumble upon an unused puddle.

In fact, those who were living most luxuriously were the first to go after civilization started to make its descent. At first, they had access to the best materials, health care, and protection but soon it became clear that their rations were not going to withstand the siege. Once the rich were left to their own devices, they did not last very long. Coddled they had grown in their lifestyles, not exposed to the depths at which the human race would dive into the pool of darkness in order to survive. Many of them resorted to taking their own lives rather than face the harsh realities of their new world.

Those who were born into this new world were not privy to the ways of the past, nor could they do much to imagine it. It always amazed the elders at how fast things changed in such little time. The young would never enjoy the simple splendors of life and would be forced to live out their days in a constant struggle for survival. No more were the days when one could look out to their peers without an ounce of worry that one of them would slit their throat in order to provide food and supplies for what remained of their families. It was the only life which the young could know, and it showed in their behavior. They were as cold to each other as the rain which fell constantly upon the earth. They knew not to speak to those they met in the wild, nor to even entertain the thought of sharing food that they were lucky enough to scrounge from the land. Comradery was no longer a part of this fallen world.

Many decided that they would live out their days in solidarity. With a complete lack of trust towards those around them, they found it easiest to isolate themselves and their loved ones. The lonesome survivors that were not blessed to have the supplies to sustain themselves did not last long in the conditions that befell them. Nor did those who decided to stay alone with their own bounties of resources, as they were quickly overtaken by others who had turned to savages willing to do anything to survive.

For this reason, there were small camps of people that decided to pocket themselves together across the desolate wasteland. They did not trust each other, nor share with one another, but it did allow them to at least retain some sense of community that had otherwise withered into the past with their previous lives. Not many of these camps were lucky enough to have a covered area to stay in. Several were simply strewn out across the dead grass in the fields, waiting for their time to come. There were a few, however, that had the fortune of living amongst the ruins of old buildings that occupied the fallen cities.

One such group clustered themselves in a building that was falling apart slowly but surely. Some of the remains of the buildings were littered with signage or sculptures that told a story of the building's past. This particular building bore no such signature. Its many rooms were drifting apart from each other like wilting petals of a flower. For years it seemed that the building would finally crumble under the harsh conditions which constantly berated it. Nonetheless, it stayed strong and served as a harbor of hope for those that grew accustomed to living their lives within its deteriorating walls.

The building was known to many of those who remained as a populous area by the standards of the new world. The building's occupants were often those who did not have any other hope of survival. Most of them were not fighters, and they did not have the ferocity to make it in a realm conquered by the type. This often resulted in unpleasant scenarios for the people in the building. Sometimes it would happen during the dead of night, but lately the marauders were ruthless enough to go in during the broad daylight. Thieves would ransack the many rooms of the building, having to fend off the other hunters for the best prizes that remained. They did not think much about the occupants of the building, who would generally bow their heads to the ground as they prayed that they would not be harmed by the intruders. Life was tough living within the walls of this asylum, but it was far more forgiving than scrapping for the remaining resources in the wild.

On this rainy day there sat a small family within one of the many rooms of that building. The father sat in the corner looking out the window, something that was part of his daily routine. The family was lucky to have a window in their room, it was one of the few rooms in the building that had that luxury. As such, they would work in shifts throughout the day looking through it to see what was going on outside the building. It also made them a target; this was not a window protected by any form of glass or structure. Rather, it was simply a hole in the wall that they had to cover with a battered blanket.

None of the family was very well kempt. They could not remember the last time they got to avail themselves of a cleaning. The two children were not born in the old world, they did not know the joys of a steaming shower accompanied by soap and shampoo. They would do what they could by sticking small containers out their window and catching the rain. It was not too successful despite the constant patter of drops against the building, they would have to choose between drinking the water or bathing themselves. Often, the necessary choice was to consume.

The father sat watching on a small wooden stool that he considered himself very fortunate to have. He sported long black hair and a blacker beard that had not seen the sharp blade of a razor in years. His tattered shirt was beginning to fall from his body as it had lost its structure long ago. He was bone thin and did not appear to have eaten much, with his ribs tempting to break through the skin on his stomach. He looked to the corner of their small concrete room and sternly barked, "Don't you fall asleep on me again Juan! I'm not pulling a double shift this time."

Juan opened his eyes with a jump in the corner of the room, he slouched against the side of the wall. His eyes were pond blue and he looked deeply back at his father, frantically looking for some excuse for why they had just been closing right before his scheduled shift. He was a young boy around the age of 14, it had become difficult for time to be kept since the fall of usable electricity. He was among the first age of children to have been born to this new world. He had been so close to enjoying the pleasures of the past, but his parents often thought that it was better he did not experience these things only to have them taken away so rapidly.

He did not stand very tall; his father was a slow grower, and it seemed that he would be the same. He was agile, however, and more than a few times his mother had to hear about his escapades from the others who lived in the building. Juan would streak around looking for trouble at times, and it was hard to blame him at a time when there was not much to do for a growing boy. Besides, his antics were not too harmful. He would often steal small things only to see the looks on the owners' faces when he would pull their possessions from behind his back and return them. It was his way of making sure that his neighbors were taking good care of their belongings.

Juan too did not have the benefit of a full set of clothes. He had recently lost one of his shoes during an incident and was very distraught over the loss of one of his finest possessions. Socks were a thing of the past as his bare toes stuck out on his one uncovered foot. He wore shorts that were laced with tears and a cloth white shirt that surprisingly had not yet been stained with mud and dirt. "I forgot that it was my turn to watch, Pops! I thought it was Mom's job to make sure everyone was on schedule around here."

Out of the other corner of the room the mother stirred from a soft nap and without opening her eyes offered, "I can't hear you, my son. Now get to work." She too was wickedly slim with thinning hair black as a raven. Her name was Stephanie, and she found what little fun she could with her family in the tiny rain filled prison that they called home. In the past she had been a teacher, and she still felt a soft spot whenever she saw young ones running around the building. Her feelings for others would never come close to how deeply she cared for her own children. She felt sorry that they were born into this world, but these were the cards that they were dealt. She hoped that she would do her best to help them along the way.

"Wait, I thought it was Teresa's turn, too! I was up all last night and I barely got a wink of sleep. That's why I must be feeling so tired now," Juan said just as the idea of deflecting the blame sparked into his head.

In the fourth corner of the room sat a little girl, Teresa, who was the youngest of all of them, being only a few years younger than Juan. She had the same caramel skin as her brother and shared the dark hair that was common throughout the family. She too had ocean blue eyes that disappeared like waves whenever she blinked. She was playing with a few doll pieces that the family had scavenged and was clearly annoyed to have been brought up, "Juan you're always telling those silly stories of yours. You just want to make someone else watch so that you can go run and play outside. Tell him I was the one who was watching all morning, Daddy!"

With that the father, Christian, glared at Juan in a way that made the young lad wish he had never opened his eyes. Christian did not have to say anything for Juan to get the message. The whole family knew that it was strictly forbidden for them to go outside the walls of their building home. Running around the halls and causing havoc was one thing, but there was real danger out in the wild. Christian was the only one who was permitted to leave the area, and that was solely for the purpose of scavenging survival equipment for the family.

"Alright, alright move aside Pops I'll start my shift now then," Juan quickly remarked in an apologetic tone. With that, the two traded places as Juan took the spot on the wooden seat and Christian retreated to the fourth corner of the room. It was not much, but they were able to make it so that all the family members had their own "personal" space within each of the room's corners. Far past were the days when a family would enjoy their lives spread out across many separate rooms of houses large enough to be fit for kings and queens. This family was more well off than most though, as they all enjoyed the pleasant experience of having sleeping bags so that they did not have to rest with their heads against the cold hard floor.

To Juan, the hours always crawled by whenever he was on watch duty. He hated having to watch the sky more than anything else in his life. He despised the way that the flicker of rain would constantly patter him in the face as he tried to look out into the abyss. The job was one that he took seriously, however, as he cared deeply for his family and knew that he was the one who was responsible for remaining alert if something went awry.

As for when something did go wrong, there was very little that the designated watcher could do to stop it. From their position in the building, the family had a view of one other building, but really, they were on the outskirts of what used to be a bustling city. Beyond that, they were able to see an interstate highway that was in terrible condition and full of holes, looking as if it would topple over any day. Past that, however, they got to enjoy one of the few remaining marvels in the area. Looking deep beyond the concrete of the extinct city, one could see a field of yellow grass that extended for a few miles before settling into the base of some trees that somehow remained standing. There were no leaves on them, but from the window it looked to be a small collection of trees making a miniscule forest. This was unheard of, as almost all the trees in the area had been cut down for weaponry and the building of the Castle.

Whenever Juan had his shifts, it was hard for him not to direct his attention solely at this forest. He wondered what kind of secrets could be held there, and why they had not cut down those trees along with all the other ones in the area. He often dreamed at night of venturing through the tall trunks and finding a civilization of people that were living unencumbered from the travesties that enveloped the remains of the world. He felt the place drawing him in with a magnetic force that he could not resist. That is why he was certain that he was going to make his way over to the forest that evening after his shift was complete.

It was a journey that he had long yearned for, and he thoughtfully planned it out too. He would go when he knew that his sister would be on watch, as there was nothing that she could do to stop him from fleeing the building. She could wake their parents quickly, but by then Juan knew his speed would have carried him well near where the highway met the beginning of the yellow grass. Out of all the kids he had encountered in his time at the building, there was no one who could run quite as fast as he could. He smiled as he imagined himself flying through the evening sky towards the forest which would hold all the answers in the world that consumed his family.

Juan knew that he would have no trouble getting out of the building and making his way towards the forest. It would not be the first time that he ventured into the outside world. His father had taken him out on walks before, during the hours of the day that were known to be the safest. Christian figured that Juan would be itching to get out of the gray building anyway, so it may as well have been under his protection. They would not stay out long, but he always noticed that Juan was staring out towards the forest that seemed to perplex everyone. Christian was well aware that Juan would do everything that he could to make it to the mysterious area one day. He hoped that day would not come anytime soon.

As for Juan's knowledge of the building and the grounds surrounding it, he felt that he had the layout memorized to exact specifications. Every time that his father would take him out of the building, Juan was busy planning exactly which route would get him to the field beyond the highway the quickest, and with the least likelihood of being seen. He understood when his family found out about his fleeing, one of them would likely go after him while the other served as a scout from the family window. Juan knew exactly which shrubs and upturned relics of old that he would hide his small figure behind as he quickly sped through the night.

As for navigating the building, it was no surprise to the family that Juan seemed to traverse the halls better than anyone else who occupied them. With all his days of sneaking around fooling with the neighbors, it made sense that Juan knew the quickest way around, and which escape routes to use when necessary. Juan was confident that he would be able to get out of the building and into the night air in under a minute's time.

In the moment, however, none of the planning that was going through Juan's head was evident to the rest of the family. He simply stared out the window, as was his job, towards that forest that kept drawing him in like a stairway descending from the vast sky. The rest of the family was huddled into their corners, not sleeping, but resting to save their energy in case of emergency. This was often the mentality and position that the family was forced to take, sitting quietly in their room.

As Juan's gaze settled into the distant forest, he hardly noticed the darkening of the sky that occurred around it. Soon, the whitish trunks of the trees stood out boldly against the dark of the night as the rain continued to drop on Juan's arms which lay on the windowsill. He enjoyed the way that time passed quickly while he was off thinking in another world, especially that evening as he anticipated his flight. When the sun finally dropped out of sight on the horizon, he turned, "Alright Teresa, no more complaints from you. I've done my time now let's see what you're about this evening."

Teresa was awake and ready for the job. It was the first time that her parents were allowing her the night shift at the window. She begged for the position for months, urging her parents to get a deep sleep while the sun was down and to save their energy for the day. She felt that she was given a greater sense of responsibility by being granted the night watch, and this made her feel mature. The night shifts always seemed more daunting; it was generally nighttime when the worst of the action was going on outside the window. With confidence, she strode out of her corner and onto the stool as Juan leapt down and returned to his corner of the room.

From there it was only a waiting game for Juan. He would let his sister get settled into the watch before making his move. He knew that she had been looking forward to this watch for a while, and so she would be extra alert to begin her shift. He also knew that Teresa had a great tendency to get tired in the evening, and although he did not know if she would fall asleep on the job, at least her senses would be lessened after putting some time into the shift. Juan pretended to sleep with his back to Teresa as she looked out the window. He could hardly refrain from twitching with joy as he thought of what was to come.

For Teresa, it began like any normal watch despite the fact that the rain was pelting down harder than usual, and she could not see the area as well as she could during the daytime. Still, she knew the zones that merited extra attention. She maintained a watchful eye over the pitch-black corners of the road and buildings that extended before her. From the corner of the room, she could hear Juan jostling around pretending to be asleep. It was far too early for her brother to be sleeping at a time when both of their parents were seemingly sleeping soundly. She was a smart girl; she knew that Juan would see her first night watch as an opportunity for him to make some trouble. Although she did not know what Juan had in mind, she knew that her first night on the job was going to be anything but routine.

As Teresa looked out into the night sky, it did not take long before she started to hear more shuffling and snickering coming from behind her. She was well prepared, with her head on a swivel. She whipped her glare back into Juan's corner just as he threw off the top corner of his sleeping bag. Juan immediately caught her gaze, and looked back at his younger sister in shock as he did not expect her to react so quickly. This threw Juan off, and he stood over his corner for an extended second before wobbling himself upright and dashing towards the doorway. All the while, Teresa stared on in amazement at how idiotic her older brother could be.

Juan dashed his way down the halls with ease, there were not many souls out in them this evening. He heard a few shouts from some of the usual night crowd as he flew by towards the stairway that would shoot him out the exit. Whenever he was out in the halls, there was a group of boys who would try to catch him and stop Juan from continuing his troublesome ways. Juan knew if they caught up to him, he would be receiving quite the beating that night instead of making his way to the forest. Fortunately for Juan, he also knew that his speed would carry him well out of the reach of the older boys, and he had the advantage of surprise on his side.

He heard them calling his name behind him as he swung himself around the stairway handrail and jumped down the last set of stairs. As he sprinted through the exit, he could hear the group behind him clamoring their way down the stairs and cursing as they stumbled over each other. Juan did not get away from the group every time, but they were too late to stop him tonight.

Juan was grinning ear to ear and started shouting with joy as he sprinted into the coolness of the night. With the darkness around him, he felt protected from being seen by the dangerous beings that patrolled the area during the evening. He knew, still, that he needed to be careful to watch his step around the building. There was no one to clean up the debris and destroyed buildings that littered the area, so there were quite a few obstacles that could ruin Juan's night. One wrong step and he would be stuck limping his way home, with not much of a chance of getting through the gang that pursued him. He did have to keep up a generous amount of speed, however, for the boys behind him had no restraints when leaving the safety of the building.

Luckily for Juan, he had all the time in the world to plan out this night. He knew the layout of the land, which he stared at for hours, like the back of his hand. Jumping through obstacles, he hit all the spots that he carefully calculated to avoid being spotted by his family who would be looking for him from their lofted home. To Juan's surprise, everything seemed to be going according to plan as he fled further from the building. He continued to hear the voices of the group behind him, but they were steadily dying down as Juan got further away. Surely, they would not be crazy enough to pursue him into the fields at this hour of night.

Juan scampered past a few wrecked cars near the highway as he continued into the dark. They were scratched up heavily, with their hoods bent up towards the dashboards. The paint that used to shine bright had dimmed greatly with the years of neglect. Juan wondered about who these cars used to belong to, and what must have happened to them when they decided to abandon their wheels on the street.

The boy never got the chance to see cars driving on the road. To him, these piles of scrap against the highway barrier were the closest thing to the automobiles of the past that he would ever see. Once or twice, he was able to get his parents to tell him stories about how people were able to get from one point to another in small amounts of time using these vehicles. Juan wished that he had a working car now to take him out to the forest, oh how that would make his trip much smoother. For now, he would have to make do with his swift legs which carried him over the barrier wall as his feet grazed against the dirt and grass that led out towards the forest.

As he continued to move through the dark evening, his memories from the past seemed to blend into what he was seeing out of his blue eyes. He could imagine the forest in the light of day. He smiled brightly in the night as his paradise grew closer with each passing lunge. No longer could he hear anything coming from behind him. The night was quiet besides the brushing sound of his shoes against the grass as he left a flattened trail behind him. His speed was increasing at a magnificent level, faster than he ever went before. He thought not about how one misstep in the gravel beneath him would send him spiraling out of control and strand him in the field which he had dreamt of traversing.

The next moments gave Juan a feeling that he was suspended in time. His heart continued to thump harder in anticipation as he closed in on his goal. His tongue swelled up; he could feel that he needed to swallow but he could not control anything besides his feet. It felt like the longest minutes of his young life as he waited in endless anticipation, wishing that his legs could carry him even faster. The crisp evening air rushed into his lungs whenever he remembered that he needed to breathe in order to keep his quest alive. As Juan began to lose full feeling in his legs, his gate began to wobble, and he realized that he was carrying himself at a speed he could not retain. In an instant, he found himself crashing to the ground and in a blur, he was covered in dirt and grass clippings. Ignoring the pain, he looked up to see that he had arrived at his destination.

When Juan looked at these trees from his window, he saw them as giants. They stood tall in a land where there was not much else that did. Up close, he saw the trees as gods. When he looked up towards them, he completely forgot about the sprint he made to reach the spot. There was no soreness in his limbs, nor heavy breathing of air flowing into his lungs. There was simply a sense of awe as Juan stood with his mouth open looking up at the wondrous sight. He could not believe the size of the trunks which were whitened and without bark. His eyes lifted towards the skies where his sight shifted to the leafless branches which delicately extended atop the trees. The thin bleached stems drifted gracefully against each other in the soft night wind.

After a few moments standing as still as a statue of the past, Juan cautiously extended a hand towards one of the trunks nearest him. He grinned as his hand laid flat against the pale wood. He felt it had a sandy and pleasant feeling to it. He was amazed at the purity of the trunk; it was one solid color that shone in contrast to the dark sky. His parents once told him that the trees used to be covered in beautiful decorations called leaves. He tried to imagine a past in which there were leaves covering these trees. He never saw a tree bearing leaves, so he did not know which color to imagine them in.

From here, Juan noticed that there were many more trees than he expected there to be. What he thought would be a contained grove which he could see right through, turned out to be a denser forest. He looked deep into the thicket of white trunks but could not see through to the other side of the night. A fear of the unknown began to creep into Juan's mind as he looked deeply into the shadowy forest of white. Curiosity overcame it, however, as he knew that he would have to continue his exploration, having come this far.

For the first time since leaving his building, Juan looked back towards his home. The building was a speck that he could hardly see amongst the sea of darkness that used to be a city. He barely made out the few windows that were on the building, and he locked in on one which he imagined was the window where he sat watching this place for hours. He wondered what his family was doing at this time, if his mother or father were standing at the window shouting his name into the abyss of night. Rain flicked into Juan's eyes as he took one last blink towards his home and turned towards the mysterious forest.

For as fast as Juan had reached this wooded area, he was moving far slower now that he had arrived. He realized he had dreamed of arriving here for so long, yet he did not think much of what he would find amongst the tall trees. For Juan, the island of bark represented an escape from the cruel world that he was being raised in, and that was enough for him to want to travel towards it. It had not dawned on him until this moment that dangers may lie within the forest, and the thought of what could be within it began to creep into his young mind.

His mind began to race as he ventured further down a dirt path that led him deeper into the forest. All he could see was the brown dirt below him, the soft white glow of the trees surrounding him, and the pitch-black darkness that seeped through the trees. He could hear the soft crumble of dirt under his single shoe. With his bare foot, he could feel specks of dirt giving way beneath his toes on every other step. Besides the gentle sounds of dirt beneath him, was the sound of nothingness. Even the constant sounds of the falling rain seemed to be muffled by the forest trees. The quiet began to harp on Juan's mind, and he thought of monstrous figures that could jump out at him from behind any of the tall trees that surrounded him. He began to hear his quickened breathing as he started to become more intimidated by his surroundings. He turned back towards whence he came, but all he could see was a parade of trees shrouded in darkness.

Worried at this point, but still determined to find his way around this place, Juan continued forward at a hastened pace. The sound of his footsteps grew louder and more frantic as he began to lengthen his stride in an attempt to find the end of the path. He wondered how much longer the forest could span. From his window, he imagined a walk through it would take only a few steps. Soon, Juan's eyes lost their grip on the dirt pathway, and he found himself clumsily running through the pale trees in order to get out of this place he once wished to enter. It was a few eerie seconds later that he stumbled into a low hanging branch and found himself face up in the dirt.

Heart beating out of his chest, Juan bolted up. He was not sure if he lost consciousness after being struck, but he was surprised to see that he had awakened in a clearing. There was a large circle of dirt around him, noticeably less trees than were scattered across the rest of the forest. As he was returning to his senses, he heard rustles from branches that he was sure were moving behind him. It was a loud crackling, as if there were a large animal dancing amongst the slender trees. Quickly, Juan's fears of the unknown lying within these woods began to crawl back into his mind. Suddenly, everything in the forest went completely still.

Juan could feel the hair on his arms beginning to stand up, a wave that progressed downwards towards his legs. He began to sweat frantically while it felt as if his body temperature dropped significantly. He shivered faintly. The air around him too seemed to drop in temperature as Juan tugged his arms towards his quivering chest. His teeth clenched and his jaw held firm in the cold air. His body felt as if it was buzzing steadily from top to bottom. He began to feel as if his spirit was leaving his body as he sat there in the cold clearing. He knew that something was behind him staring a hole through the back of his head. Juan slammed his eyes shut in fear for a brief moment but could not resist the urge to turn around.

Regaining a sense of feeling, the boy swung himself around as he braced himself with his hands clenched in fists and held high in front of his face. Slowly, he heard the soft dirt twirl around him as he directed himself, eyes still closed, to where he heard the noise coming from. It was now silent throughout the dark forest as Juan forced his eyes open to see what beast had come to visit him. Alas, when his vision refocused, he could see only the white trees swinging amongst the gloom. His eyes darted around, knowing that he had heard something from the area he was now staring at in disbelief. Even more dark thoughts popped into the child's head, knowing now that there was something out there which could see him, but he could not see himself. He stood for a second longer staring forward into the murky abyss while his heart began to settle down. Then he heard a twig snap from right behind him.

Surprising himself by how fast he was able to take action, Juan leapt around with a fist held high in the air. He was ready to bring it down in a furious strike upon whatever was stalking him through the forest on that fateful night. His eyes were not in focus as he brought his fist towards a small figure that had appeared behind him. Right as he was about to make contact with the shape, he heard loudly, "Stop!" By some grace, Juan was able to stop his fist from flying into the face which he now saw to be his younger sister's.

Teresa stood there in the clearing with her massive blue eyes glued to the fist of Juan that had stopped just short of smashing into them. She had a worried look on her face, her lips trembling as she lowered her hands which were going to be too late to rescue her. Coming to her senses, she lifted her tiny arms back up and flung away Juan's fist and replaced it with a relentless jab to the side of the stunned Juan's stomach. "What are you doing throwing fists at your sister in the middle of the scary woods!" she yelled as she continued to pound Juan, who could not comprehend what was going on.

After a few more blows, Juan caught her, "What the hell are you doing out here? You are supposed to be keeping watch back at the place. Didn't you wake up Mom and Dad and tell them that I ran away?" Juan looked around the clearing frantically, wondering where his parents could be now. Surely, they would not have let his young sister come out to the forest alone to look for him.

"I didn't wake them up! I knew you were going to be up to something while I was making my first night watch, so I followed you out here. You thought you would be too fast for anyone to keep up with, but you haven't seen me running!" Teresa squeaked at him as she struggled out of his grip.

Juan could not believe that anyone, let alone his sister, could have followed him out to the forest at the speed at which he was going. This was not something he planned for, and now he was worried that he would be putting both his life and his sister's in danger. Not to mention that their home was being left unguarded while their parents slept. He knew that he needed to be a strong leader to get them out of this dark forest and back to their home safely. There was no telling what the road back would have in store for them, in a world where madness ran fluid. "We need to get back home," he said as he started to walk with his sister out of the forest.

As they walked back looking for the dirt path that had brought him into the clearing, Juan remained cautious. He knew it was not his sister that was lurking amongst the trees, the sounds made were much too loud to be her small stature. His head was on a swivel as Teresa suggested that they take the route out she had found. Within a few minutes, the two were back out of the forest and under the moonlight, looking towards their home in the rubble city in the distance.

They did not say much as they trotted back at a steady pace towards their home. Both of them were thinking of how angry their parents would be when they woke up to find that their children were missing during the midnight hours. Teresa worried that she would never be given the opportunity to keep watch during the night again. Juan was upset that his actions would get his sister into trouble. The two of them had no difficulty keeping up with each other as they gently treaded back through the field.

After a few minutes they were within sight of their building, appalled at the scenario that was developing before their eyes. At the base of the building, they could see orange flames beginning to creep up the sides of the remaining structure. There was a group of at least 10 people surrounding the building and waving their arms around, throwing bottles at the entrance before explosions sparked into the air. The sound of glass shattering against the hard concrete building filled the area. The kids began to hear the yells and screams of many inside the building, worried for their lives. They looked to see if anyone was in their home's window, but could not see anything.

Worried, the children scampered to cover behind one of the cars on the highway as they looked on at the devastation which was engulfing their home. It was not uncommon for raids to be conducted in the night, but they had never seen this many raiders at once. Further, these new fire bringing tools were foreign to the assaults. The bottles were continuously being thrown with force against the building, and the fire kept rising through the rain, which was proving futile in combatting the ascending flames. The worst part for the children was that there was nothing they could do to help their family. They were not strong enough to take on or even distract a militia of this size.

The kids did not recognize the assailants that stood outside their burning home. This was not too surprising, however, as many times they were not able to get a good look at their building's attackers. Their father instructed them that whenever they saw an attack going on during their shifts at the window, they were to alert the family and then get down. Their father did mention to them that there were a few small gangs that had formed throughout the city and that they wore certain colors to represent their people, but it was too dark in the evening to make out what the attackers were wearing.

All appeared to be lost as the building continued to be set ablaze, with the attackers making their way through the doorway and entering the homes of the inhabitants. The shrieks from within the building grew louder and carried throughout the night sky and the entire city. The children, still huddled by the highway, were forced to cover their ears as they heard what they were certain to be the deaths of their neighbors and perhaps even their parents.

As the children were about to close their weeping eyes and lay down on the cold road, they heard different howls coming from the building. These were no longer cries for help, but instead they held the force of ferocious battle cries.

Quickly, the raiders that had entered the building were tumbling back out of it. They were being chased by men and women who lived in the building and who were armed with weapons such as sharpened sticks, shovels, and axes. There had to be at least 50 people charging from their homes to defend their property together. In addition, the people with windows in their homes began hurling rocks and nails at the invaders who remained outside the building. The invaders quickly realized that they had picked the wrong building on this cold rainy evening.

With confidence, the defenders poured out into the night street protecting their home. It was the first time that they had worked together and fought back against threats, but one could not tell by looking at them. Their tactics were sure, and they fought seamlessly amongst one another as neighbors that cared for their home and those that resided within. It did not take long before screams of victory were chanted as the crowd realized their numbers advantage and began to drive their weapons through the hearts of their enemies.

They did not have it in them on that night to show mercy to the ones who were trying to burn down their home. Pent up frustration and anger overcame the fighters, and they felt only pride in defending their families. For too long, the group had worked as scared mice who would run from the lions that would stalk outside their home. Now, they were learning that they could fight back with force and strength in numbers. Dressed in rain and scarlet blood, the people worked together to find hope.

Eventually, Juan and Teresa found the strength to open their eyes again after it seemed that the action had died down. They did not know what to expect as they looked towards the place they no longer expected to be a livable home. Slowly, their eyes crept open and they saw a group coming towards them holding weapons that were dripping in blood. Frightened, they both moved to dash away before glancing towards the group once more and realizing they recognized them. As the rain poured down, Christian and Stephanie dropped their weapons in a clash and extended their arms towards their scared children. Drenched in the bloody night, the family embraced.

Far off in the distance, amongst the fields that looked onward into the broken city, there stood a castle. It was dark, built with piles of well-molded stone that were imported from the far reaches of the world. The smooth stone was built high up into towers that peaked deep into the cloudy sky. While the castle was amongst the largest structures remaining on the planet, it was pitch black against the backdrop of the evening and could hardly be seen from the exterior. A massive stone door led to the interior of the building, held up by huge wrought iron chains. There were only a few visible windows from the front of the castle, and it was rare to see any light shining from within them. The place was guarded by many men who made use of all the most dangerous weaponry that was still available. They stood silently with automatic rifles and rocket propelled grenade launchers as the showers continued to pour throughout the night.

The men stood confidently, knowing that their weapons would never see action. They had never come across any group that had weaponry that could combat that which they equipped. The few groups in the area that did have some form of weaponry had been hunted by these guards long ago and they became victims of the mass weapon eradication in the area. Whenever the guards heard word about someone who was displaying power, they would be hunted down within a few days' time. Their ruler wanted to make sure there was no possible way that he could be defeated. For this reason, the men stood tall in the rain, knowing that they would not have to worry about blurred vision in the event of a raid on their castle.

The halls of the castle were well guarded. Guards stood with machine guns crossing their chests at the entrance of every door. The halls extended deeply throughout the castle and there lay a bright red carpet draped across the floor of the walkways. Each hallway had around three entrances that led to rooms which were mostly bare and unused. The castle looked from the outside to be monstrous and gigantic, but the majority of the inside remained hollow. Nonetheless, guards were instructed to remain at their posts throughout the entirety of the day. They were given very little time outside of their shifts, but they enjoyed living safely in the cellars of the castle and the regular meals that they were fed.

The dining hall was the largest room that the castle held. It loomed massive and held dozens of rows of tables and chairs hand crafted from the finest oak wood that could be found in the barren land. Swinging from the ceiling were two giant brass chandeliers, another artifact of the past gone nearly extinct. It was a respected place; the guards ate in an orderly fashion during their allotted times and never took more than their fill. In the dining hall, guests would quickly forget about the horrors that engulfed the world as they were swept away to a place where they could focus on rejuvenation and simpler times. As most of the guards were of age to remember the past, this would often be the spot they would go to reminisce about their former lives.

For such a grand hall, the meals had to be fit for the occasion as well. These were prepared by several chefs who were constantly working in the kitchens. All of them were renowned chefs at some point in their past. They found ways to enjoy themselves while creating new meals for their hungry company. This was likely the best stocked kitchen that remained in existence, with silverware and cookware of the past filling the shelves from floor to ceiling. The chefs too did not get the pleasure of much free time, needing to be on duty for three meals a day, but they got to eat well and also had living quarters amongst the cellars.

The only person who was permitted to keep their home in the above ground portion of the castle was its owner, the tyrant. On this rainy evening, the tyrant stood looking out into the rainy abyss through a large glass window that occupied his room. He was working through his usual routine, which involved staring out the window for hours and pondering which moves should be his next. He saw himself as a leader of many, trying to navigate them through a world which he was working to cleanse of harm.

For as long as the tyrant could remember, he was focused on doing what he thought the world needed most. In the beginning, he served as a symbol of hope to the people. One that would help them overcome all the earthly issues that they confronted. By the end, however, those around him started to misunderstand his mission and turned against him in a way that threatened the fabric of society. His castle, which was once a symbol of peace, was turned into a feared monument. On this evening, he wished not to dwell on the past and what he had done to make it to where he stood now.

Thus, the tyrant waited with unblinking cocoa brown eyes as the rain tapped the window just inches away from his face. He was a tall man, standing a few inches above six feet with long lean limbs. He had long brown hair that dipped below his shoulders and a lengthy beard to match it. Despite the length of his hair, he did not give off the appearance of one who was unkempt. With his bounty of care products, he was able to attain a cleaner look than most during these trying times.

The tyrant wore a black button-down shirt that was securely buttoned up to the neck. The shirt was tucked into a pair of slim black jeans that rested above a pair of leather black sandals. He stood at the window with the candles unlit, looking as dark as the night sky. Struggling to keep the past out of his thoughts during this rainy evening, the tyrant backed away from the window slowly and closed his eyes.

When he opened them, he looked around and saw the room that he had built for himself. The room was larger than most of the other rooms throughout the castle. It stood high with dark purple walls that seemed to trap whatever light came through the window throughout the day. There was not much on the walls in terms of décor, aside from a stuffed buck mount that hung over the large bed. The antlers of the beast extended high towards the ceiling of the dark place as its pitch-black eyes stared forward for eternity. Directly within the buck's gaze was a mahogany dresser that was worn down but still stood sturdy, though it held nothing on its top shelf. On a small table standing by the window, there was a lamp that too was likely one of the few remaining in existence. It had a copper stem with a beige top and was rarely used.

The tyrant, tired from the day's thought as he often was, slowly made his way over to the mahogany dresser. It was one of the first things he brought into the castle after its construction was completed. He was grateful as he rubbed his hand along the smooth top surface wondering how many others had the honor of owning such a fine piece of artwork. He paused and stopped his hand as he drew closer to the end of the dresser. In the body of the dresser, there were six drawers that could be pulled out. The tyrant slowly brought his hand towards the gold handle of the drawer at the top right. Smooth as silk, the drawer slid out of the dresser and revealed a cream-colored envelope that sat alone in the middle of the space.

Calmly, the tyrant moved his hand towards the envelope, being careful to keep it in its pristine condition. He grasped it and began to bring his hand from within the drawer as he closed it back up. Holding the envelope now, he brought it in front of his face, close enough so that he could see the words scribbled on the front of the envelope in the dim room: "To James".

15
Remember

It was late in the year, and the trees had evolved to embrace hues of deep orange, red, and yellow. Birds flew throughout the trees and sang joyously as they seemed to be chasing each other around in an avian play that humans could never fully grasp. Small squirrels bounced from tree to tree as they harvested bulbous acorns and prepared to bury them in the ground to help the squirrels withstand the hunger of a long winter ahead. White tailed deer pranced through the lush forest brush making hardly a noise as they nomadically danced to the next grazing spot.

The animals of the forest collectively turned their necks in an instant as they heard the low volume zoom of a dark blue car drifting along the road next to their home. Almost instantly, the rain started to fall more heavily on the creatures. Slowly, they began to make their way towards their homes for shelter to wait out the worsening storm.

The man noticed the forest around him grow quiet as he continued to drive himself and his son along the road he had traveled many times. "It'll do us both some good to get out of the house for a bit, James. You know I've been busy with this new work project, and I know you've been worried about those school assignments piling up. That's probably why you've been acting this way lately, it's all just a part of growing up and you will get through it. Trust me on that," the man said as he looked to his son, hopeful that some of the words he spoke were getting through to the boy. The boy said nothing in return, staring ahead at the road as the rain splashed against the windshield before being swept aside by the rampant slide of the wipers.

The past few years had been difficult for the man and his wife. He remembered the first few years of his son's life being peaceful and full of joy. The child was seemingly obedient, never crying or starting up commotions. He would go to bed when he was put down and he would stay quiet until his parents came to retrieve him in the mornings. People would remark on how lucky the family was to have such a wise and kind child growing up with them.

Things started to become more difficult when the child came of age so that he could move around on his own. His silent demeanor remained the same, but he would often find himself in troublesome situations. Things started to break around the house, valuable items such as family heirlooms that the man and woman held in high regard. The boy started to hit people that would try to pick him up or play with him. When it was time for the boy to begin schooling, he had trouble connecting with his classmates, and often spent his time alone in the classroom throughout the day. Despite a loving family at home, there were signs that the young boy was not fitting in with society as he developed.

This became even more apparent when he got to middle school. Before, the child would mostly keep to his own devices, but by this time he began to wreak havoc upon those around him. He became somewhat of a troublemaker in his classes, realizing that this would help him to get the attention of those around him. He routinely mocked teachers, bullied other students, and skipped classes in order to leave the school and find more misfortune. Recently, the man and woman had received a call from one of his teachers telling them that the child was seen pulling girls' hair as he walked them around the school ordering them to do things for him.

This worried the man and woman; they were not sure why the child was resorting to this type of outlandish behavior. When they were children, they thought themselves to be polite and respectful to those around them. They could not recall a time when they were troublemakers, at least not to the level that their son was behaving. Still, they hoped that their son would grow out of this phase and begin to feel a greater sense of appreciation for the things that he had in his life. That is why the man planned to take his son out on the trails during his rainy day off. He wanted to try to connect more with the boy and get a sense of how he was feeling. Problematically, most attempts to reach out to the child were shut down by a lack of willingness to communicate on the child's part.

The trails that they were headed to were not too far from their home. They were a collection of muddy veins that ran through a hilly region beyond the area that the newly constructed Sadie & Gunther's occupied. The man still recoiled in disgust whenever he passed by the place on the way out to the trails. The trails were a place that the man had visited frequently in the past when he was at the peak of his fitness. He loved to run through the miles of different pathways and would also take his bike out whenever the weather allowed for it. Though he visited these trails many times, there were still countless routes throughout the area that he had yet to explore.

Another thing he loved about the area was the abundance of animal life that seemed to thrive throughout it. While the city and the area surrounding it had become congested with the developments and buildings that he himself helped to erect, he felt peace in the nature that was still untouched by the growing civilization. As he traveled around the trails, he would always be careful not to disrupt the way of life that the many animals living there had grown accustomed to. He knew that this was their home, and he respected that. In the back of his mind, he worried about the day when people would decide to extend even further into nature with the inventions of man. He could hardly blame anyone besides himself, the one responsible for making it possible for such construction to occur.

As he drove forward, continuing to get further away from the sounds of the city, the man thought back to his views before he became a father. He thought that fatherhood would bring mainly joyful moments. Of course, there would be ups and downs when raising a child, but he thought his knowledge that he was raising a good person would get him through the tough stretches. Now, he was not so sure of that. The man remained hopeful as a father, but he did not prepare himself for the difficulties that stemmed from his son's behavior of late. The fact that his son could be someone who found joy in others' pain was beyond the stretches of the man's imagination. He continued to question why his son was acting in such a way.

As the pair continued deeper into the forest, the rain began to pick up, and the lines on the road began to blur. Rain smashed against every inch of the windshield as the wipers struggled to keep up with the steady flow. Besides the sound of the heavy rain, the car remained silent for the remainder of the ride. The child was not one for sparking up conversation, and the man had to adjust his focus solely on the road ahead. In a few more minutes, the man thankfully pulled into a dirt parking lot nestled by the side of the road.

After struggling to pull into a spot amidst the showers, the man finally turned off the car and looked to his son. "Good thing I brought the rain jackets!" he said with a smile and laugh as he turned to the backseat to produce two bright yellow jackets. With the amount that it rained in the area, the car never left the house without them sitting in the back seat. As the two began to shove their arms through the coats, the child began to speak up.

"Why are we doing this right now?"

"A little rain won't stop us, we need to clear our minds a bit," responded the man.

"You know that's not going to work. I don't want to be here with you, and I know you'd rather be off doing something for work. We're only here because Mom forced you to take me while I'm suspended," the boy said with fierce eyes.

"That's not true James, I want nothing more than to be here with you today. I want to understand how you're feeling, and I want to help make things better for us both. This is a place I've come to many times when I'm searching for answers to life's many problems," the man replied calmly.

"There's no problem with me!" screamed the child, "The school is the one with the problem along with everyone that goes there. You should see the way that I am treated when

I don't act out, it's like I hardly even exist. I stand in the corners watching the days go by as those around me are content to forget about who I am. I want them to recognize that I am here and one of them."

"I feel your frustrations, son," the man said somberly as he tried to extend his right hand to comfort the boy. "Trust me that you will find your purpose, and you will find those that are happy to recognize you for the person that you are. In the eyes of your loved ones, you are everything to us. Think about your mother, your grandparents, and I, there is nothing that we would not do to make you happy."

The boy rejected his father's hand, swiping it away, "I just don't understand why they treat me differently." With a dejected look, the boy opened the car door and jumped out into the rain. The man sighed from his car seat as he watched the boy lifting his hands to his eyes as the rain poured down around him. Puddles surrounded the child's feet, and to the man looking on it appeared as if his son were hovering gently over the water. The boy took his hood down and raised his eyes to the sky, feeling as if submerged amongst millions of falling raindrops.

"Hey! Keep that hood on, we don't want you getting sick!" the man said as he leapt out of the car. The child did not listen. With a splash, the man hustled over to his son who was still staring up into the sky as if seeing something magnificent. The man shook the boy as he ripped up his hood, shielding the boy's head from the relentless rain. With that, the boy looked at the man angrily and started walking away towards the forest path. The man followed.

For a while, they walked in a line with the boy leading the man down pathways he had never encountered. The man was content with this, he knew the route that they were going down and wanted to see where his son's imagination would take them. He could sense that the boy was still heated from their earlier interaction, so he had no problem with the silence that enveloped them. No one else seemed to be out on the trails that day, which were quiet other than the sound of the rain splashing against the muddy path. Their boots scattered mud in all directions as they continued to trek deeper into the trees.

After walking about a mile down the brown trail, the man was about ready to call it quits and tell the boy it was time to head back to the car. The rain was crushing them in the forest, with their only respite being the dense leafy tops of the trees above them. Suddenly, from the forest there came a squeal from an animal. It was a high-pitched cry, one that displayed surprise and deep pain. It sounded as if it came from nearby, to the left of the path. For the first time during the walk, the boy lifted his head from its downward position towards his own feet. He jolted it to the left of the path, curious as to what the source of the yelp was. Before the man could say anything, the boy was tumbling through brush trying to get a glimpse of the distressed creature.

The man was not so quick to react and before he knew it, he lost sight of the boy and was crashing through the bushes with low visibility. He yelled out for his son, but he could hardly hear himself over the drapes of rain. When the boy did not respond, the man continued onwards in the direction he had seen him plunge. For another 100 yards or so, the man suffered through cuts and scratches from the local flora. Finally, he came to a clearing where he saw his son huddled over a figure on the ground.

The man ran over to the boy and put his arms around his shoulders. "Come on James! You know you can't run away into the woods like that. You just about gave me a heart attack. What's gotten into you!"

The boy stared towards the figure as if he did not hear a word that the man spoke. He was transfixed with whatever it was that made the cry for help. The man slowly looked towards the limp body and recognized it as a deer laying down in the mud. It was a beautiful looking buck with pitch black eyes that were still blinking slowly. It had long horns that extended in multiple points far beyond the body of the beast. Its mouth hung open displaying teeth that looked fresh and white against its pink tongue. The deer's pelt was chestnut brown, looking as if it had been cleaned thoroughly by the rain. Amongst the pelt were small pea sized dots that shone white through the precipitation.

Without having heard the cry of the deer before, one may have simply thought that the creature was laying down for a nap amidst the rain. The buck laid calmly looking up at the man and boy with its eyes shimmering like an eight ball. There were no jerks of the legs or sounds of anguish, just the patter of the rain splashing against the brown animal. It did not take long, however, for the two to determine what it was that made the buck cry out for help.

Downward towards the leg of the deer, right above the hoof, there was an arrow sticking out of the flesh. The light brown fur was splattered with the deer's vibrant red blood. So too was the grass that surrounded the area in which the deer lay, and the pool of blood was continuing to spill over quickly. The arrowhead extended a few inches from the deer's leg, and it was still connected to the back of the arrow which bore red feathers. As the two stared at the deer in disbelief, once more it began to whimper begging for assistance.

This was the first time that the man and boy had come across an animal in need like this. They were used to seeing helpless animals who had already been killed on the road, but never did they see a deer crying out for their assistance. Surely, the situation was not looking good for this buck, but the man surmised that the wound was not drastic enough that the deer would die on that rainy day. He began to think of what he could do to help when the boy interrupted.

"This is awesome! A free kill for us, we didn't even have to bring gear or anything. I've always wanted to go hunting, Dad. Let's finish it off here and then haul it back so that we can hang the head up at the house!" He looked down at the buck with a bloodthirsty glare in his eyes. It was clear that he did not see the remaining life in this creature, but rather the opportunities that the deer could bring to him in death.

The man looked at his son with more disbelief than he had while looking at the injured buck. His heart hurt to hear the boy speak with such cruelty as he yelled, "What are you talking about son! This buck is full of life, this wound isn't going to keep it off its feet for too long. You don't want to kill this beast and hang it when we have the opportunity to save its life!" As he yelled at the boy, the man thought of the first aid kit that he always kept in his car. It was not meant for this kind of situation, but it would have to do. No longer trusting the boy to be around the buck on his own after hearing his comments, the man tossed his keys over. "Go run to the car and get the med kit out of the back. I'll wait here and make sure everything is stable."

With a frown, the boy snatched the keys out of the sky and started to lumber back through the woods following the path of trampled brush. As the boy disappeared from sight, the man looked towards the buck laying gracefully in front of him. He looked up towards the sky and felt the raindrops striking him in the eyes. He anguished over how his son could have such hate in his heart to want to kill and hang this animal that lay in need of help. It would be one thing if the boy wanted to end the buck's suffering, instead he was focused on what he could gain personally.

The man stood in silence with the rain dressing him as he thought about the struggles that his son was going through early in life. He felt empathy towards the boy, and though he knew not why his son was choosing this disruptive life path, he was overwhelmed by the feeling of needing to help him change his ways. The man realized he did not know what it meant to be a good man, nor did he know what it would take for him to raise his son into one. He talked about being a good man and he tried to be one, but it remained a title without a clear definition. Standing with the injured buck in the pouring rain, he felt that his heart would lead him and his son along the right journey. His mouth curled into a slight smile as he turned back towards where his son had leapt from the clearing in time to see him stumbling back with the medical supplies.

The architect snatched the bag out of the sky as his son passed it over to him and retook his place standing over the injured buck. He was used to building and creating things with his hands, not providing medical relief to those in need. Unsure of himself, he bent over the buck which made a slight lurch towards him with its legs. The man decided that his duty was to get the arrow out of this creature's leg. Slowly, he extended his hands towards the area where the arrow protruded from. He noticed that the wood of the arrow was flimsy, and he determined that he would be able to snap off the arrowhead and the feathers so that he could pull the rest of the wood through the deer's leg. With firm hands, he snapped the ends off the arrow as the buck kicked its legs around wildly.

He knew that as soon as the arrow was dislodged, blood would begin to pour from the open wound. Thus, he made his way towards the medical bag and brought out gauze, antibiotic ointment, needle, and thread. The buck lay twitching at his feet as he worried that he was hurting the beast rather than helping. The man took a deep breath as he grasped the remaining part of the arrow and began pulling it through the back of the buck's leg. It did not come easily, with the buck thrashing and threatening to impale him or the boy with its large antlers. "Get back!" the man yelled to the boy who was finally obedient to his father's command.

As the buck whined deeply into the stormy sky, the remainder of the arrow was fully removed from its flesh. The buck's legs kept writhing in pain as a sea of blood began to spill out over the man's hand. Quickly, he tossed the fragment of the arrow aside and took a glob of the antibiotic ointment to his finger. He thrust it towards the buck's open wound as he wondered what kinds of diseases this beast may hold. Nonetheless, he continued to try and clean out the area as the buck continued to dance in pain beneath him. All the while, the boy continued to stare on in awe as the man worked.

Suddenly, the man felt the throws of the buck beneath him begin to simmer down. It felt as if the animal finally understood that the man was trying to help it. That, or the pain medication he administered was soothing the beast of its pain. At this point, the man was not thinking so much about what he was doing but rather just letting his body react to the moment. Having sown little in his life, he took a grab at the needle and thread which were meant to provide stitching support on humans in emergency situations. He had no idea whether they would have the same effect on the brown furred deer.

With a deep breath and a prayer, he threaded the wire through the small eye of the needle and plunged it into the dime sized wound that was continuing to gush bright blood. The deer reacted with a quick jolt, but it was surprisingly calm for this invasive tactic. For the next few moments, the man used the stitches to close the wound on both sides of the leg, hoping that the deer would not get itself into any trouble and rupture the wound once again. The bleeding diminished greatly as the man continued to work with his blood-soaked hands. The rain washed the blood away from them in brief moments so that he could see his skin, only to be covered up again with red in the blink of an eye.

Soon, with the wound looking far better than it did when the two arrived on the scene, the buck began to lower its eyes and appeared to be entering a tranquil state. The man gently applied more of the antibiotic ointment to the inflicted areas as he reached for the gauze to wrap around the injured leg. Many times, he draped the white thin lace around the leg until he felt it sufficient, at which point he cut the white fabric and placed some tape around the edges to keep it from falling off too quickly. Surely, this material was not meant to be on a deer which was jumping throughout the forest. The hope was that it would somehow help the beast to survive a bit longer in the rainy landscape until its leg could heal naturally.

With the work seemingly complete and the deer left in a sedated state, the man began to pack up the medical bag. He found a few wipes to try and get the rest of the blood off his hands before zipping the bag shut. At that, he looked up from the ground at his son who seemed as if he had not blinked throughout the whole ordeal. The man smiled as he looked at his son standing and watching him in the rain. The man stood up slowly and patted the boy on the shoulder, "Let's let this one rest for now, we've done all that we can to help." With that, the two took one last look at the calm brown buck whose eyes were still open, appearing to be looking up at each of them. The boy gave a pat to one of the buck's long antlers and the man turned away and went back in the direction they had come from.

The rain continued to fall on the pair as they returned to the path and started to head back towards the car after their eventful day. "Thanks for that, Dad. What you did was pretty awesome back there. I had no idea you had skills like that!" the boy chirped at the man as they continued walking side by side.

The man looked at his son in surprise. He could not remember the last time that his son had looked up to him in such a fashion. It brought him great joy to think that he may have taught his son an unexpected lesson in the woods that day. He hoped that it could leave the boy with a sense of respect for the lives of those around him, whether they be human lives or those of the animals. "I didn't know I had those abilities either, son. I just did what felt right to me in the moment. There's something that I want to make clear to you, James. The answers to life's questions are not always obvious. Many times, I myself have stewed over which direction is the right one to take. Back there, there were many paths we could have chosen to go down. We could have followed your advice and put the beast out of its misery, we could have left it there to die in this storm. I tried not to overthink our decision, instead I acted. The lines between right and wrong are often blurred. It is not often that you will be gifted instructions on which method is the best. Most important is to make the decision that you feel in your heart is the correct one, and to follow it through. If your decision proves to be the incorrect one, do not let it get you down but instead strive to be better."

With that, the boy gave the man a nod and they continued onwards through the drenched forest. Before long they arrived back at the car where they got in squeakily against the leather seats. They buckled up quickly and the windshield wipers awoke from their slumber, jumping back into a furious glide across the glass. The man was not sure whether the things he said would resonate with the boy, or whether they made particular sense. All that he could do was remain hopeful as they made their way back down the road.

Silence

The tyrant brought one hand to his face and wiped tears from his eyes as he closed the letter he held in the other. He delicately laid the letter back in the drawer of the dresser which he closed shut. He stood there for a few moments with his eyes closed, silently reflecting on his memories. The next time he opened his eyes, there was a faint glow coming from the window. The morning had arrived.

Shocked that time had slipped away from him in what felt like such a short period, the tyrant slowly made his way over to the window. He wanted to get a glimpse of the world that he created. The barren wastelands that seemed to hold no life, no hope for a brighter future. Recently he had begun to question whether all that he had done to get here would put the world together in the way he wanted.

When he got to the window, he looked up at the sky which remained a faint gray. It was still early morning, the flat desolate landscape slowly waking up with the rising sun. The tyrant frowned, squinting his eyes and moving his forehead towards the glass paneling of the window. Out in the fields beyond the castle gates, there were a pair of strong, lengthy antlers bouncing around in the clearing almost joyfully. As if it knew nothing of what the world had become, a young buck danced mightily beneath the clouded sky.

Miles away from the castle, the flower shaped building remained intact. The morning sun crept up behind it slowly, casting shadows beneath the building. There was an eerie calmness in the air despite the hectic nature of the evening prior. The bodies of the invaders still laid out strewn around the building forming a sort of fleshy wall. One by one, the members of the building began to shuffle out of its main entrance. They started to work on moving the bodies further out towards the fields. The decision was that they would bury them there.

As more of the building's community began to flow out into the streets, there was a sense of peace between them. They could not quite put a finger on it, but they could all tell that there was something different about today. It was not just that they were working together to remove bodies from their front lawn, something they had never done, but there was something that remained foreign to them.

As the morning continued onward, neighbors became acquainted with each other. They found themselves deep in conversation with those whom they previously discounted as close living adversaries. The elders talked about what they remembered of the past. The young sprinted around the nearby streets laughing and chasing one another.

It was as if all at once that the people who remained realized what was so different about the day. In unison, they pointed their heads towards the sky and looked upward. The rain had ceased.